"Wyatt, no!"

Elsie's scream registered at the same moment Wyatt felt something hard slam into his head. Blinded by the pain, he threw his arms out, tried to find someone to fight back, but darkness was already closing in. No, no, no, he could not afford to pass out right now.

"Elsie, run!" he yelled before he went to his knees, the explosion of pain echoing through his entire head. He struggled to maintain consciousness, and after a second or two managed to stand back up. In the chaos, he'd lost track of Elsie, his assailant, Willow the K-9, everyone.

Wyatt started down the trail. As he ran, he winced against the throbs of pain and held a hand to his forehead. Shiny blood streaked his palm.

Where. Was. Elsie.

That was what concerned him most. Whoever was after her was still somewhere on the island. Right now, very close to her. Pursuing her.

Unless...they'd just caught her.

Sarah Varland lives in Alaska with her husband, John, their two boys and their dogs. Her passion for books comes from her mom; her love for suspense comes from her dad, who has spent a career in law enforcement. When she's not writing, she's often found dog mushing, hiking, reading, kayaking, drinking coffee or enjoying other Alaskan adventures with her family.

Books by Sarah Varland

Love Inspired Suspense

Treasure Point Secrets
Tundra Threat
Cold Case Witness
Silent Night Shadows
Perilous Homecoming
Mountain Refuge
Alaskan Hideout
Alaskan Ambush
Alaskan Christmas Cold Case
Alaska Secrets
Alaskan Mountain Attack
Alaskan Mountain Search
Alaskan Wilderness Rescue

Visit the Author Profile page at LoveInspired.com.

ALASKAN WILDERNESS RESCUE

SARAH VARLAND

LOVE INSPIRED SUSPENSE
INSPIRATIONAL ROMANCE

LOVE INSPIRED® SUSPENSE
INSPIRATIONAL ROMANCE

Recycling programs for this product may not exist in your area.

ISBN-13: 978-1-335-59786-1

Alaskan Wilderness Rescue

Copyright © 2024 by Sarah Varland

For questions and comments about the quality of this book, please contact us at CustomerService@Harlequin.com.

Love Inspired
22 Adelaide St. West, 41st Floor
Toronto, Ontario M5H 4E3, Canada
www.LoveInspired.com

Printed in U.S.A.

O lord, thou hast searched me, and known me.
—*Psalm* 139:1

To God, the One Who showed me how much stories matter. To my family, for your support and your love. To my students, who do a fantastic job asking if my book is done yet when I'm on a deadline. And to my dogs, you've taught me more than I could ever say.

ONE

Waves splashed onto the rocky coast of the remote Alaskan coastline that Elsie Montgomery called home, their predictable pattern usually able to ease her mind. No matter what, the waves rolled in and out, soothing in their regularity, something she desperately needed today. Elsie hated days that didn't go as planned, when she wasn't *enough*. Instead of tearstained faces mixed with smiles, there would be eyes avoiding glances, hushed words. Spoken and unspoken apologies for something out of all of their control.

Today's search and rescue mission had turned into a recovery. It always felt like a personal defeat.

But Elsie had dealt with them before, she reminded herself as she dug her hands into her husky Willow's fur. She needed the softness of it between her fingers, something to ground herself in this moment as her heartbeat pounded and she started to fight against the tightness in her chest. She hated failure, hated to lose…

Was it worse on the heels of yesterday's success? She didn't know. She sat by the shore until the sunshine faded into late summer night. A glance at her watch showed ten o'clock, time for her to go inside. Her body needed to rest, even if her mind refused to shut down. It might be another long night of crossword puzzles and a mug full of hot Tang.

Elsie eased open the door of her cabin, loving the low creak it made. Partially because it was nostalgic, old-fashioned and made her feel connected to the cabin, which had been built well over fifty years ago. And partially because, practically speaking, it made it difficult for someone to break in without her hearing them. Not that that was a major concern, but Elsie lived alone and liked to be prepared for all contingencies, so she couldn't help but think it.

She walked to the kitchen, pausing to pour a glass of water, and glanced down at today's newspaper while she took a long sip. "Local Woman and Dog Rescue Missing Five-Year-Old." In the photo, her smiling face was pressed against Willow's. She hated the publicity, but her best friend, Lindsay, a journalist for the local newspaper, had reminded her that the family wanted to celebrate, and she was allowing them to do so when she gave the interview and permission for a picture.

She poured Willow a bowl of dog food and watched, her mind wandering, while the dog ate her well-deserved meal.

Elsie had consented to the article, but it didn't mean she liked the spotlight. Something in her almost recoiled from the attention. It was enough to know that what she did mattered, that she and Willow had helped find someone else who had been lost. Because if there was anything Elsie understood, it was being lost.

Of course, that had been years ago...being abandoned

on an island many nautical miles away from here, closer to Kodiak Island than Homer, found almost coinciden-tally, because someone had happened to be fishing in a remote area. By all logic, she should have died when she was three years old, wearing her too-big purple rain jacket, alone in the Alaskan wilderness. But someone had found her. Maybe that was why Elsie had decided to dedicate her life to rescuing others who were lost. She knew, with all that was within her, what that was like.

If only she understood the concept of being found as easily...

Desperate to put her thoughts anywhere besides today's failed rescue mission and her own past, she walked to her bedroom. She'd skipped dinner, but the protein bar she'd eaten earlier had quelled her hunger. Besides, the unease inside her wouldn't let her eat.

She could call Lindsay. Her best friend since child-hood, Lindsay lived on the other side of the bay, where the town was. Most people lived there, though Elsie and a few others had cabins or houses in this more remote area. Her friend had questioned her when she'd decided to buy her small cabin after high school graduation with money she'd saved working in the summers, rather than stay in town. Elsie hadn't had a good answer for why she craved the space. She simply knew that the cabin was the only home she could afford—it had needed significant repairs but she'd been able to accomplish those over time—and that ultimately she felt safer out-side, among the tall spruce trees and wilderness, than she did in a town, even a small one. It bothered her in some ways that she felt like this. And she wondered, as she did with most things that she didn't understand,

if it was tied to her past. To her time on the remote island. And what had come before.

Elsie climbed into bed and reached for the novel that
sat on her bedside table. Agatha Christie. Somehow an
old mystery on a day like today made everything make
more sense.

Prayer probably would, too... She could practically
hear Lindsay's voice saying it, not with judgment but
with a smile. A reminder intended to help. After Elsie
had been rescued from the island and had been hauled
from Children's Services office to Children's Services
office, she'd gone into foster care in town, Destruction
Point, Alaska. The small town was a boat or plane ride
from Homer, Alaska, just beyond the town of Seldovia.
Her foster parents had lived next door to a family with
two kids close to Elsie's age, Lindsay and her insuf-
ferable older brother, Wyatt. She'd spent enough time
with their family to be exposed to their faith, something
that was important to Lindsay and her parents, though
maybe not Wyatt.

Elsie had always tried to be polite about their faith,
though she didn't understand it. She knew it concerned
her friend, though she couldn't quite understand why.
She was respectful of Lindsay's beliefs. Lindsay never
seemed judgmental about it, only...sad?

Another topic she didn't want to think about tonight.
She flipped onto her side and turned the book's pages
until she reached her spot.

Usually she could lose herself in a book, but Elsie
struggled to focus. Beside her, Willow wasn't as relaxed
as usual, either, periodically raising her head to look

around the room as though she were expecting something to happen.

"You can't wind down, either, huh? You're okay, girl. Go to sleep." She reached down and ruffled the fur on the dog's neck, but the husky didn't relax into the mattress as she usually would have. Instead her muscles felt tense under Elsie's hands, as though she was ready to spring into action.

"What is it?" Elsie whispered, feeling her own muscles tense in response. This dog was more than a pet or even a work partner. Willow was her lifeline in the wilderness, her eyes and ears. Elsie herself was not unskilled in tracking or wilderness survival skills, but it was Willow's senses and perception that made them an incredible team, well-known for their track record of finding people during those golden hours when survival was still likely. Elsie, like most human searchers, had too many thoughts during a search, the clock ticking from the moment someone disappeared. Three weeks without food, three days without water, three hours without shelter in extreme weather conditions. Willow didn't have to worry about that, didn't have that kind of noise crowding her brain. In essence, dogs didn't overthink. They used their noses, their senses, their training, and they did their job nearly flawlessly. In all her years of K-9 search and rescue—a decade at this point—Elsie had never seen a dog make a wrong decision. Their instincts, especially Willow's instincts, were dependable.

Which was why when Willow stood and started to growl, chills chased down Elsie's spine. Then the low, slow creak of the heavy wooden door confirmed it.

Someone was inside her cabin.

Elsie swallowed hard against the pounding of her heart, made herself breathe deeply. Slow everything down. Painstakingly, conscious of every shift of her body, every movement that could potentially make noise and alert someone to her presence, she set her book on the nightstand, then reached to turn off the bedside table lamp. Willow's eyes were just as effective in the dark as the light, and Elsie hoped it might put whoever was inside her house at a disadvantage.

She herself preferred the darkness also. It was so much easier to hide.

Flashes of something stirred in her mind. A memory of a memory of a dream? More like a nightmare. It was like an impression of darkness. A closet? Gnawing hunger in her stomach. Hiding. Hoping no one would find her.

The thought—memory?—distressed her. Elsie had always wanted to be found…hadn't she? Didn't everyone?

She slipped off the bed onto the floor, feeling her way along the wall, debating whether to wait here or move toward the hallway.

Willow had stopped growling. She had positioned herself between Elsie and the door. To move anywhere else in the house would put them both in even more danger. So she waited.

A creak on the floorboards, and Elsie was certain the sound was moving away from her. She risked tiptoeing back toward the bedside table and grabbed her phone. Shielding the brightness of the screen from the doorway, she texted Lindsay.

Someone's inside my house. Going to try to call 911.

Then she pressed the numbers 9-1—

Creaking. Closer.

She pressed another 1, then set the phone facedown.

"911, what's your emergency?…911…what's…?" The voice was muffled by the carpet, then by the pillow Elsie dropped on top of it.

"Stop hiding, Elsie. We were always going to find you. You were never supposed to survive. It's time to stop hiding now." The voice was a man's. Low, rough, nondescript.

No one she recognized.

Willow leaned forward in the darkness, and when Elsie reached out a hand, she could feel the dog's body begin to shake.

Elsie took a slow breath in. Let it out.

Willow yelped.

Elsie tried to run, but it was too late. Hands clasped her face. She fought, struggled, until they moved to her neck, started to tighten. She let out a scream.

Snarling. Growling.

This time it was the intruder who yelped, his hands coming loose from Elsie's neck. Willow, trained in protection as well as search and rescue, was doing well.

But Elsie's neck throbbed and panic nearly paralyzed her. Willow might be trained for this, but she wasn't.

Please let 911 have sent someone on the way… She prayed, for the first time she could remember, and continued to fight against the darkness, scrambling away from the intruder and hoping she'd be able to hide from him until help arrived.

Wyatt listened to the dispatcher's voice on the radio as he finished off a bowl of after-dinner cereal. Working as a contract pilot for the Alaska State Troopers and several other organizations meant that it was useful to know what was happening in the area. Besides, it wasn't like he had anything else going on. It was listen to the radio or sit on the couch doing nothing. Eat. Sleep. Work. He needed to get a life. At least, that was what his sister told him every time they talked. She didn't understand that he couldn't risk going back to his old life, partying, only caring about himself. It was easier to just…be alone.

"But maybe I need a few friends or a hobby or something," he said as he carried his bowl to the sink. There had to be a balance between who he'd been in high school and the decade beyond and…this. He was thirty-one and living like an eighty-year-old hermit.

Sven, his massive brown malamute, groaned from his place on the couch.

"Yeah, you're my friend, I know."

He could have sworn the dog rolled his eyes as he flopped onto his other side, leaving another patch of dog hair on the couch. Eat. Sleep. Work. Clean up after his dog. That was a more accurate summary of Wyatt's life.

The radio crackled again.

Female resident reporting distress. West side of the bay, Destruction Point…

Wyatt sat up straighter.

Elsie.

Surely not, he tried to tell himself as he hurried from the couch to pull on his boots and jacket. Behind him, Sven grumbled with interest.

"You have to stay. I'll be back soon." His first thought had been for Elsie, but it could just as likely be one of the older retirees who lived out that way. Still, his sister's friendship with Elsie made her come to mind first. No matter who was in trouble, Wyatt knew it was likely he could beat the police there. Besides, if there was some kind of scale, Wyatt could use as many good deeds tipping out his previous bad ones as possible.

He was out the door and to his dock in seconds. The boat roared to life without issue—something that couldn't always be said for it—and he started off across the bay. It wasn't a wide body of water, just enough to be separated from the main part of town, functionally speaking. He tried to breathe deeply as he navigated the waves. The ocean wasn't too rough tonight, but the spray drenched the bow of his boat as he cut across the water as fast as he dared in the growing darkness.

Elsie's cabin stood just at the edge of the woods, close enough to have an unobstructed view of the ocean, but far enough away that even the most dramatic tides didn't reach it. He thought he remembered Lindsay telling him once that the cabin was a century old. He couldn't imagine building something, doing something, that would last that long. Her cabin was someone's legacy, tangible and still standing. Did anything in his life have half a chance of outliving him, besides maybe the terrible reputation he'd worked to earn in his younger years for going through women and alcohol like a chain-smoker went through cigarettes?

Forcing himself away from that thought spiral, he beached the boat, tied it down and hurried to her cabin.

The front door was ajar. He crept inside, wishing he'd taken time to grab a weapon, but he hadn't been thinking clearly when he left. Hopefully the years he'd spent in outdoor pursuits had honed his muscles enough that he could still hold his own in a fight. He hadn't been in one in half a decade and had never thought he'd need the skills again. Wyatt sure hoped they'd show up for him if he needed them now.

Indecision gripped him as he stood still, letting his eyes adjust to the darkness. Should he call out to her? Or try to surprise whoever was in the house?

Because the fact that 911 had been called for someone in this area, added to the fact that her door had been opened... Wyatt no longer thought he was overreacting. Making a split-second decision, he went with this second option, moving forward slowly, conscious of how easy it would be to step in such a way that the old wooden floor creaked under his steps.

"Where are you?" a voice called out, drawing out the vowels in a way that put Wyatt in mind of childhood nightmares.

Shivers chased down his spine. This was more than a random occurrence, and that thought caused the terror in his stomach to turn cold and icy.

Rather than focus on how it made him feel, he moved toward the voice. The cabin didn't look big from the outside, but the layout made the most of the space, rooms connecting to each other in a way that older settlers in Alaska had been fond of. Many of these cabins had loft areas, too—was that where Elsie's bedroom would be? Chances were good she'd been asleep when someone broke in...

He moved into another room, movement up ahead catching his attention. A silhouette that sent shivers up his spine. Someone was stalking her, hunting her in her own house.

Why? Who?

No time. He had to stop them.

He heard a dog's low growl and then a snarl.

Wyatt ran forward in time to see the silhouette drop. He launched himself on top of the man, letting his fists fly, relishing the pain in his knuckles as they connected with the other man's jaw.

He caught movement out of the corner of his eye and thought it might be another assailant, but quickly realized it was Elsie. "Elsie, run!" he yelled at her.

"Wyatt?" Her voice was perplexed, shaking and colored with fear.

The attacker chose that moment, when Wyatt was distracted by her voice, to hit hard—hard enough to stun Wyatt momentarily. The man rolled out from under him and started to run.

The dog growled.

"Willow, stay."

Wyatt took off after the man through the maze of the cabin and out the front door. The attacker had a head start and seemed to know where he was going. He peeled off into the woods. Wyatt followed for as long as he could, feet pounding the earth, until he finally had to admit he'd lost the trail. His breathing ragged, he forced himself to admit what he knew to be true.

The man was gone.

He kicked the ground and bit back a word he hadn't used in years.

Noise behind him made him swivel his head to look up. It was Elsie and her dog.

"Wyatt?" So many questions in her voice and in the way she said his name.

He didn't have answers. Instead he said, "I'm sorry I lost him."

"It's okay. It wasn't… It's not your problem."

"Do you know who it was?"

She hesitated. He saw her face, as though she were debating her answer, but then she slowly shook her head. It was odd. He almost felt like she was lying. But she'd have no reason to, right? Especially not about something like this, with her safety on the line. Still…

"You sure you don't?" He pushed anyway, wanting the truth.

"I don't think I've ever seen him before. Not that I remember, anyway."

There was something odd in that statement that he wanted to come back to, but now wasn't the time.

His gaze had moved to Willow. "Your dog tracks people, correct? Lost people?" He thought he'd heard something like that.

She nodded.

"Technically I lost the trail. Could she…?"

"She could. But I don't want to ask her to. It's too dangerous for her."

"Dangerous for *her*? Someone attacked you tonight. We have to find out who."

"*We* don't *have* to do anything," she said firmly, more so than he was used to hearing her talk. He'd always thought of Elsie as his sister's delicate little friend. She was petite, barely came to his shoulders, and slight enough that it seemed if the wind kicked up too hard, it could probably blow her away.

Her voice was anything but delicate right now.

"Elsie, please."

She sighed deeply, then bent toward the dog. She leaned close, buried her hands in the dog's fur and pressed their foreheads together, then stood up slowly.

He didn't think she'd said anything out loud to the dog, but Willow took off.

"If my dog gets hurt, I'm holding you responsible."

Yeah, because it was *his* fault he could have gotten his own self killed trying to protect her from whoever had been trying to attack her.

She didn't exactly seem grateful. Of course, to be fair, she hadn't invited him here. He'd headed over himself with hardly thinking it through.

They hurried through the woods after the dog. She stayed in their line of sight, but it was still exhausting trying to keep up with the husky, who ran over roots and obstacles with grace while Wyatt found himself stumbling, exhaustion making him clumsier than usual.

Finally, the dog let out a howl, one that reverberated with a melancholy that reminded Wyatt more of a wolf than a dog.

"She lost the trail, too," Elsie translated.

They hurried to her side, emerging from the shadows of the woods onto the beach that made up the other side of Destruction Point.

Wyatt moved closer to the water and thought he could make out marks in the beach. Footprints or boat prints—it was impossible to say with the texture of the sand. "He may have had a boat waiting. So he intentionally targeted you. This wasn't a crime of opportunity or he'd have had a boat in front of your house somewhere."

"It looks like that." Her voice was flat. Frustrated. Fearful but not surprised.

That was what had caught him off guard earlier. With all the emotions he was picking up on, surprise wasn't one of them.

Shouldn't it be?

"Were you expecting someone to come after you?"

She was looking off into the mist, into the darkness. Somehow it seemed to him as if she was *part* of the darkness. Wyatt felt a shiver run down his spine.

"I don't know that I'd say I was expecting it…"

"That's the second time you've talked to me in riddles tonight, Montgomery." In high school, he'd called her by her last name because it seemed to annoy her. It did the trick and got her attention now. She turned to him with a frown, stormy gray-green eyes flashing.

At least he'd drawn some kind of anger out of her. Someone who was attacked in her own home with no warning *should* be angry. Wyatt was angry. Elsie seemed afraid, sure, but mostly she seemed resigned.

Like it was inevitable. He didn't understand.

She let out a breath. "Come on. Let's go back to my cabin. If you want, I'll make you a cup of coffee and give you the best explanation I've got. Seems like the least I can do."

It wasn't quite a heartfelt declaration of thanks for coming to her rescue, but it was something. Considering their relationship had never been smooth, normal or one of mutual caring, it was probably the best Wyatt could hope for.

"Sounds good. Lead the way."

She turned and headed back into the woods, seeming to be more at home in the dark on these trails than most people would have been in the day.

She feared the person who'd come after her, but not the dark. Not the wilderness.

Elsie Montgomery was stronger than he'd realized. She may not be the person he'd thought she was after all.

He'd complained his whole life that people judged him without knowing him. At some point, he'd gotten tired of trying to be better and let himself become the person they imagined. It was who he was even now, when he knew this wasn't who he wanted to be.

What about Elsie? Who was she?

TWO

Knowing Wyatt had been inside her house was almost as strange as having someone break into it without her permission. At least her would-be attacker wasn't someone she would ever see again. Or she hoped not. Wyatt was in and out of her life in at least a casual way because of their connection to Lindsay. She usually saw him during holidays like Thanksgiving and Christmas, but the two of them made it a point to avoid each other.

Even though he wasn't someone whose opinion Elsie would have said mattered to her…he apparently was, because she found herself wondering what he thought about the small cabin. Most people wouldn't be impressed, with its small size and simple layout, but it was her refuge.

What would Wyatt think of it? And of her? Lindsay had said more than once that the cabin was a reflection of who she was as a person. Minimalistic, but warm and cozy. Simple, but with unexpected details.

The front door opened into the main area, which was warm with the wood tones of the walls. A small kitchen sat in one corner, and opposite that was a stone fireplace, with stones that reached for the vaulted ceiling. Initially the cabin had had a low roof that was sinking in and needed to be replaced, and Elsie had wanted as much of a natural feeling to the cabin as possible. It was earthy and comfortable. Traditional. And it was the only home Elsie had ever had that was worthy of the word.

"Coffee?" she offered, and Wyatt nodded, saying nothing as he looked around. Elsie busied herself with the coffee maker to avoid seeing his reaction to the space.

"Cream? Sugar?" she asked.

"Sugar would be great. I used to drink it black, 'cause I figured that was the manly thing to do. Hated the stuff." Wyatt laughed at himself. He had a different laugh from what she remembered. Easy and a little self-deprecating. Looking up, Elsie watched him as he walked toward the fireplace, then took in the built-in bookshelves against one wall, the cozy chair she'd situated in the corner for the best views. He looked so large in her cabin. She'd forgotten how tall he was. Over six feet, maybe by a couple of inches.

"I like your place," he said at last. "It feels like a home."

A spark caught in her heart at the word *home*. Exactly what she'd been going for, since it was all she'd ever really longed for. The compliment made her chest warm, her heart skip a little. Only because of the way it complimented her, not at all because the implication was that if he liked her house, then…

He must like who she was, too?

No, that would be silly, and she was a grown woman, not really given to silliness. There was no time for it. There were too many people to find.

Or was she avoiding finding herself, facing herself?

Too deep for tonight. Elsie shoved the thought back and yanked the carafe out, even though the coffee hadn't finished brewing, realizing as she did so that she hadn't responded to Wyatt's compliment.

"Um, thanks. I really like it here."

Yeah, that was brilliant. Strange that she didn't have people over more often, with stunning displays of wit like that.

She added sugar to the coffee, something that made her smile a little. She'd definitely have pegged Wyatt as a black-coffee kind of guy, all swagger and projected toughness, but the longer she was around him, the less he seemed like the guy she'd known in high school. Or thought she'd known.

"Here you go," she offered, holding out a pottery mug to him.

"Thanks."

She took her own coffee, made with a splash of half-and-half and no sugar, and motioned to the small table by the side window. "Have a seat."

Normally, she found the darkness outside beautiful, but as soon as she sat down, Elsie wondered if someone was out there watching. She set her coffee down on the table and reached to shut the curtains, blocking out the view. It felt like a small defeat, like she was letting whoever was after her win. But she had to be practical. Leaving the shades open was an unnecessary risk.

"Weird to think they could be out there, huh?" Wyatt commented, and Elsie nodded, exhaling the breath she hadn't realized she was holding as she did so.

"It's not my favorite feeling, wondering if I'm being watched."

"Have you had that a lot?"

Elsie looked up at him, considered. "The feeling of being watched?" she asked to clarify.

He nodded.

"It's happened before."

His expression made it clear he didn't like that answer. "Is this recent, or something that's been going on for a while?"

"Recent." She didn't know if that truth made her feel better or not. It seemed to indicate that whatever danger she might currently be in was something that had a starting point. Therefore, it might have an end point, right? Now that she thought about it, she'd started feeling this way in the last couple of weeks. What was going to happen next?

"You didn't seem very surprised that someone was after you."

"I'm not." She seemed to be on a brutally honest streak here. Not that Elsie condoned lying, but she'd have anticipated at least dancing around the truth with someone like Wyatt. But nothing about him made her feel uneasy or defensive tonight.

That alone should terrify her. That was probably how he'd ended up dating half the girls in his senior class, spending more than his fair share of time out at the end of Destruction Point Road in the dark with some of them, too, if rumors were to be believed. When she'd been young and naive, Elsie had harbored the notion once that she could change him and had nurtured the tiniest crush on him.

Time and his continued bad behavior had killed that, thankfully. It was too embarrassing even to admit to herself. Sweet, quiet Elsie with a crush on the town bad boy? It was so cliché and impractical it made her cringe.

Now this grown-up version of Wyatt was here, handsome as ever but with a note of humility and self-awareness that he hadn't possessed back in high school. When had he changed? Had she avoided him so studiously every time they'd crossed paths recently that she'd missed this?

"What can you tell me? Are you in trouble somehow?"

She quirked her mouth into a smile. "It seems like it."

"You know what I mean. Are you…I don't know… mixed up in something?"

"We sound like our collective mystery-solving experience is Nancy Drew books."

"Add that to a couple of criminal-investigation shows I like to watch on the weekends and that's pretty much what I've got."

"No way am I supposed to believe you used to read Nancy Drew."

Wyatt grinned, shrugged. Then his face grew serious. "Really, Elsie. You're in danger. I want to know why."

"And I said I'd tell you what I know…" She trailed off, wishing she hadn't made such a foolish promise. "But why? Is this just curiosity? How are you going to help?"

"I have no idea. I fly for the Troopers sometimes. Maybe they could help?"

"They've got nothing to go on. And besides, I don't want to involve the Troopers."

"Why?"

"Too much drama. I don't want to be caught up in all of that. Someone broke in. Maybe they tried to steal something and just needed me out of the way. I don't see any reason to think I'd be a target."

"Except?"

"You know that I was in foster care when I lived next door to you, right?"

Wyatt shook his head.

Stuck in his own little world even as a kid? Elsie knew he'd been around when she and Lindsay had talked about it. She referred to her foster parents as "my foster mom" and "my foster dad." Surely he'd heard her say those phrases at some point over all the dinners she'd spent at his family's house?

Her expression must have shown her disbelief.

"So I wasn't an observant kid."

"Anyway, when I was in foster care…" She hesitated. Maybe it was the fact that it was so easy to talk to him, or that he didn't seem intimidating. Or like it wasn't such a bad idea to have a crush on him anymore. Maybe she was overly emotional from what had happened tonight. All Elsie knew was that she was finding herself distressingly attracted to this man and therefore needed to hit the brakes on any more vulnerability. He'd seen the inside of her cabin. He knew she was in danger.

She couldn't keep giving him glimpses into who she was. It wasn't *safe* for someone to know you that well. Her foster family had taken good care of her, but they'd never tried to form much of an emotional connection to her. She'd always understood that she could count on food and shelter, but she'd never felt loved or known. Maybe that was a good thing, though, because the idea of allowing either was utterly terrifying to Elsie.

Opening up to Wyatt any more was scary. At the

same time, she'd said she would tell him what she knew. Didn't she owe him that? She could abbreviate the story.

"I was in foster care because my parents were out of the picture. There's a chance something…less than legal…could have taken place surrounding that whole situation." Elsie shrugged, but she could tell that Wyatt saw through her pretended nonchalance.

"You don't know for sure, though? That your biological parents were into something illegal?"

"I don't know any details of why I ended up not being with my parents." There, that sidestepped his question a bit but still told the truth.

"So someone could have been after you this whole time? That doesn't make sense. Why come after you now after however many years? Surely if they'd wanted to abduct you or something, they could have done that before now."

"I know. It just crossed my mind, but it's definitely unlikely." She said the words with more assurance than she felt. It was unlikely, but not impossible. She'd always been uncomfortable with the lack of detail surrounding her past and her childhood, but that didn't mean there was *actually* anything criminal that had gone on. More than likely it was the same-old-same-old story of parents who picked an addiction over a kid, the Office of Children's Services took over and details got lost by the time a child grew up and started asking questions.

Except…usually kids didn't end up found on remote islands, alone. Too traumatized by…something to help rescuers and authorities understand anything that had happened to her before her rescue. And if her past was really as cut-and-dried as she was trying to fool herself into thinking it could be, shouldn't she have answers by now?

Still, Elsie didn't want to pursue this line of thought with Wyatt here. She'd told him she'd explain why she'd been suspicious. She'd held up her end of the deal and she had zero desire to stand around convincing him that she was in danger. She didn't need anyone butting into her life.

Something about her too-innocent expression made Wyatt wonder what else there was to this story, but he was uncomfortable prying any further into Elsie's life. It had been a heedless impulse to come here in the first place, a random desire not to stand aside while someone got hurt. More specifically, he hadn't wanted to risk Elsie being the one who got hurt when he could do something about it.

His instincts had been right that she'd been in trouble. Were his instincts right about something else going on, too? That she was still in danger and that she might know more than she was letting on?

"I still think we should let the Troopers know what happened. Or at least Destruction Point Police. They should be on their way."

Elsie raised an eyebrow, and yeah, he got it. The Destruction Point Police Department consisted of three men, one patrol car, two old bicycles and a boat that made the bicycles look high-tech. Not that they were incompetent; one of his best friends was on the force. But it was a very small town with the resources to match and not a lot of crime beyond the occasional bar fight or domestic dispute, which was usually resolvable by one of the pastors of the two local churches. Elsie was talking about a decades-old ordeal. No way would they have the resources to look into that.

But why not let the Troopers investigate? Was she trying to protect her privacy? Wyatt had picked up on her discomfort just having him in her house.

The last thing he wanted to do was push her into something that made her uncomfortable.

"Do you honestly think this was random?" He took another sip of coffee and studied her as she considered the question. Before he'd decided to be a pilot and focus all his energy there, he'd done better in his few college classes than his family had expected. His psychology classes had been his favorite. He enjoyed reading people, something he'd probably used for negative purposes once upon a time.

Elsie's facial expression didn't change, but her eyes did focus on some point beyond him for a long moment before she met his eyes again. "I don't think getting the Troopers involved will help either way. And I think there's definitely a good chance it's random."

Not the answer that would help him sleep well at night, but one that could probably let him walk away and leave her to the privacy she clearly wanted. He nodded once.

"I appreciate that you came over here. I still don't get why you did, but I appreciate it. I wouldn't have expected it." She was usually so polished, it was odd to hear her stumble through her speech like this.

"I had to, once I heard it on the radio. I wondered if it was you." He looked away from her, not sure what she'd see in his eyes otherwise. Any kind of interest on his part would be unwelcome, he knew. She deserved so much better than him. "Law enforcement should be here soon," he finally said after searching for a topic. "What's taking them so long?"

Elsie shook her head. "Maybe they got here when we were in the woods and went to search?"

Seconds later, a knock on the door seemed to confirm her theory. Especially when they heard a voice say, "Destruction Point Police."

With one last look in his direction, one that seemed to remind him that she didn't want a big deal made of this, Elsie started toward the door.

"I'll stick around till they leave and then head out, if that's okay."

She met his eyes, nodded and then pulled the door open.

"Elsie. Thank goodness." Seth Winters, one of the local police officers, had been in Wyatt's graduating class. He was an overall good guy. Probably Wyatt's favorite of the officers, so he was glad he was the one to respond. "When I got here earlier no one answered. I did a sweep of the area but wanted to check your house again." He seemed to be visually scanning her for injuries. "You're not hurt?"

"No, I'm okay. They got away, though, whoever broke in. Wyatt and I tried to chase them down, but…" She shrugged, as if to finish her sentence nonverbally.

Seth's gaze swung to Wyatt, seeing him for the first time. His eyebrows rose. "What are you doing here?"

Suspicious because he was law enforcement and Wyatt had been first to the scene of a crime? Or was there something between him and Elsie? He couldn't see the second working. Seth was a decent guy, nice, honest, honorable, the kind Elsie deserved. But somehow, Wyatt thought they would make a terrible couple.

"He heard on radio traffic and came to check on me." She spoke up before he could, and while Wyatt didn't feel like he wanted someone else fighting his battles for him, he appreciated the fact that Elsie was willing to stick up for him. And it helped to ease his mind a bit about her and Seth. If she was defending Wyatt, then chances were good she wasn't falling for the other guy's too-concerned demeanor.

"That so?"

"You accusing me of lying, Officer, or accusing Elsie?" He raised his eyebrows.

The other man didn't justify Wyatt's snark with a response, which he kind of appreciated. Instead he turned to Elsie.

"I'm going to send a team here to get fingerprints and see if any other material evidence was left behind."

"No, you don't have to do that," Elsie said.

"Good idea," Wyatt said over her. She turned to him and glared. He saw irritation and a warning to be quiet in her look.

"It's procedure. After that, we can start a search for who it might have been and so on. It's possible trace evidence was left that could help us identify—"

Elsie spoke up. "Do you have to investigate fingerprints and all of that if I don't want you to?"

Wyatt looked at her in surprise, noticing out of the corner of his eye that Seth had done the same. Finally, something they could agree on.

"Why?" the officer asked.

Wyatt kept his mouth shut. Just watched Elsie. Waited. Kind of wanted to pray for her to make the right choice, but getting back onto speaking terms with God after all the ways he'd messed up his life in the years previous was harder than he'd thought it would be.

Would God even listen to him?

Help her, he finally tried, sending the plea heavenward as he waited for whatever she would say.

"Tonight was awful," she started, looking away from both of them and reaching down to pet her dog, who had settled at her feet. "But I think it was an isolated incident. I don't want more people in my house combing over it, analyzing things that may or may not help us find whoever was responsible. It was probably a crime of opportunity."

Wyatt stared at her. That was the opposite of what she'd admitted to him earlier.

Seth apparently didn't notice the tension in her jaw, the way she was avoiding both their eyes. He continued, trying to explain typical protocol. "Fingerprints and further investigation are what we always do."

"Can I waive my right to those? Turn them down?"

The officer sighed and Wyatt felt it down to his soul. "Yes."

"I'd like to do that."

Elsie smiled at Seth. "Thank you so much for being ready to investigate." She turned to Wyatt. "And thank you for risking your life for someone you've barely talked to in years. I appreciate it more than I can say."

Her tone clearly communicated that she was ready for them both to leave. They were being politely dismissed. Seth Winters opened his mouth, then shook his head and started to the door, clearly sensing that this was a losing battle.

"Wyatt…" Elsie said. He had a feeling she was about to kick him out a little more directly. Probably because she didn't want him to call her out for the inconsistency in her story.

Before she could say anything further, he asked, "I, uh, could I use your bathroom before I leave?"

"Sure. It's that way." She motioned down a small hallway off the living room. Wyatt walked that direction, despite the fact that he didn't need it. What he needed was to kill a bit of time until the police officer left so he could talk to Elsie alone.

When he came back into the living room a minute later, she raised her eyebrows at him.

"Did you really just want to wait till he'd left?" The corners of her mouth were tugging into a smile.

Wyatt shrugged. "Maybe. Listen, let me help you, at least. I get it if you don't want police involved. That would be intrusive. But you admitted earlier that this might not have been random, and the place the guy left his boat tells me the same. Let me help you."

"And you wouldn't be intrusive?"

"I'm the lesser of two evils."

"Bet no one's ever said that about you before."

He jerked his head up, half-offended, and realized she was joking. Teasing.

Certainly not flirting?

He didn't know how he'd begin to process that. Elsie was the last woman he'd expect to flirt with him, and despite the fact that she was gorgeous, he would never want just a fling with her. He wasn't that guy anymore, the one who didn't take anything seriously and knew what to say to get a woman interested for the short term.

Besides, he wanted her to know that he meant his offer of help.

Maybe, though, he had messed up too badly to ever change the way people thought about him.

THREE

If anyone would have appreciated a little intentional flirting to distract from a stressful night, Elsie would have thought it was Wyatt.

Instead he'd either ignored her lighthearted teasing or seemed almost offended, if the tightness in his jaw and around his eyes was any indication.

Huh. First coming here to help her, with no ulterior motive that she could discern. Now refusing to flirt back. She thought he flirted with every woman he met. Maybe she didn't know Wyatt at all. At least, not *this* Wyatt. Maybe time had changed him, and why not? It was unfair to assume that he was the same person he'd been in high school.

"Hey," she tried again, "I really appreciate your willingness to help. And like I said, I'm really thankful you came over, but..."

"Yeah, you don't want to pursue it. And I'm probably the last person whose help you would want."

No arguments there. But not because he'd been a player in high school. That had been years ago. It was that she didn't know him, didn't want him intruding in her life any more than she wanted a police officer prying. Keeping in mind how tense he'd seemed when she'd tried to flirt with him, she wanted to reassure him and explain herself. But Elsie didn't lie, not even to spare people's feelings, so she kept her mouth closed.

"I'm glad you're safe." Wyatt walked to the door, looked back at her once and stared at her with an intensity that burned and warmed her at the same time. "Please be careful. I'm worried about you, Elsie."

And before she could respond, he opened the door and disappeared into the darkness.

Elsie blinked a few times, then locked the door behind him. She didn't know how she'd wanted that odd encounter to end, and it was too late at night to figure out how she felt about any of this. For now, she'd send Lindsay a quick text letting her know she was okay, and tomorrow, she'd call her. Talking to her friend always helped her clarify what she was thinking and feeling. And right now the topic she was confused about her feelings on was...Wyatt.

Would that be weird, to talk to Lindsay about her brother? Just as soon as she wondered that, Elsie dismissed the concern. Lindsay would know she wasn't thinking about Wyatt romantically.

Still on edge, Elsie checked the lock on the front door again. She could have sworn she had locked it before she'd gone to bed, but someone had broken in anyway. Still, it was funny how her desire to be in control dictated that she make sure the door was locked. She turned off the light, waited a second until her eyes adjusted and then walked through the small main area of the cabin, checking windows. All locked. She should be safe. Alone.

For once the idea of being alone didn't appeal to her. She wondered, only briefly, what would have happened if she hadn't all but chased Wyatt out. If she hadn't refused to discuss his offer to help her. Would he have stayed for a while, maybe sat on the couch and had another cup of coffee, helped her wind down from the night? Just because he wasn't the kind of man she would ever date—she could barely imagine what kind of man she *would* date—didn't mean they couldn't be friends. Right?

She blew out a breath. He'd left, and it was her fault. She was alone in her cabin in the woods, with the lingering reminder of how many people had invaded this space tonight.

Which brought her back to her most-uninvited guest— the would-be…what? Abductor? Murderer?

What was his motive? She'd love to pretend it was a break-in gone wrong, that the intruder had made up threats that meant nothing. But she could find no evidence that anything had been stolen. She was forced to conclude that he'd been after her personally. The threatening words *had* been real and had likely tied to something in her past. Somehow.

She pulled the covers up to straighten them, then tugged them back and climbed into bed, thinking that Wyatt was more correct than he'd realized. She'd probably been in real danger. But at the same time, Elsie was convinced she was right, too—this had to be a one-time thing. She had no idea why anyone would come after her in the first place, much less attempt to do so again. Even if this whole thing was tied to her past, she wasn't any kind of high-value target, wasn't important or famous. Her photo and interview in the local paper was the closest to a claim to fame she had. And people didn't abduct search and rescue workers in the happy aftermath of a successful rescue.

She thought again about his threatening words, the way he'd implied she was his target. That didn't have to mean it would happen again. It couldn't. And what if it wasn't targeted at all? What if something like human trafficking was at play here? Then the threatening words had just been to frighten her, maybe subdue her into cooperating.

Ignoring the niggle in the back of her mind that said she was being too optimistic, and entirely too creative in her interpretation of what had happened, she tugged the covers up to her chin and called for Willow. The dog trotted easily into the bedroom and jumped with a grace Elsie envied up onto the bed. She settled herself down, her weight comforting to Elsie, who felt her breath ease and steady.

Was she entirely foolish to hope that she would wake up tomorrow to a normal life? And what did it say about her that human trafficking sounded less terrifying than other interpretations of her situation?

She'd rather face something awful like that than have this be related to her past in any way.

Almost without warning, she was cold, cold the way a three-year-old child would be if left in the elements of a rainy Alaskan summer day. She could feel beneath her hands the rock of the jagged ocean-side cliff where she'd taken shelter. Elsie could feel nothing else. No emotions, no sense of abandonment, anger or loss, just...nothing.

She'd seen counselors over the years, several of them

because none had ever really stuck, and they'd had different explanations for her sense of emotional nothingness connected to her past. Elsie didn't need to know why. She didn't want to dig back into her old life at all.

If this situation required her to…

Wyatt was right—he was one of the last people she would want involved.

All through high school, she'd admired him from a safe distance. It was practically expected that she'd have at least a little bit of a crush on her best friend's brother. And he'd always been unfairly attractive with his broad shoulders, sandy hair and easy smile. But she didn't trust him.

Of course, the Wyatt of her memory had been selfish and never would have risked his own safety and comfort to come to her rescue in the middle of the night. Wyatt *had* done that tonight, so maybe Elsie didn't know him. But that didn't put him on the list of people she'd want to rehash her past with.

Telling him what she had tonight had been enough, even if her vague explanation of being in foster care wasn't the same as the full truth.

She had no idea who she was. She'd been a Jane Doe as a toddler, unable to be reunited with her birth parents no matter how much people had tried.

All through high school, people had treated her like she was fragile because of her petite size and generally quiet and compliant disposition, but Wyatt had *especially* treated her like that. Instead of being one of the girls who was thought of as an adventurer, brave in her own right, people had treated Elsie like she might break. She'd spent her adult life proving that she was more capable than her size and delicate features made it seem. She *knew* she was capable. Strong. Tough.

But if she had to dive back into whatever had happened in her childhood, she didn't know if she could keep being that person.

And she couldn't stand to imagine investigating with Wyatt and maybe at some point seeing pity in his eyes. She didn't want his pity.

Despite willing herself to go to sleep, she lay awake for hours. Anxiously wondering who could have been after her and why.

And remembering the flicker of hurt on Wyatt's face when she'd all but sent him away when he'd only wanted to help her.

It was going to take some strong coffee for Wyatt to make it through this day on as little sleep as he'd gotten lately. He'd been overwhelmed his whole boat ride back to town, imagining Elsie alone in that little cabin, wondering who was after her and why, wishing he'd done things differently in his life so he could be the kind of man Elsie would trust.

It was basically a recipe for not sleeping when he'd gotten home and finally crawled into bed that first night. Sven hadn't seemed to mind Wyatt's sleeplessness. No matter how many times he rolled over, tugged the covers this way and that, the massive malamute had stayed asleep, his heavy body like the best kind of weighted blanket.

If only Wyatt had slept that well.

The next night hadn't been much better. During the day he stayed busy enough, but when he tried to fall asleep at night he worried about Elsie. Wondered what it was that made her so hesitant to accept help from him or anyone else.

Maybe he'd text her today. He didn't have her number, but his sister would.

Pulling his mind away from Elsie, Wyatt made his breakfast and checked his schedule for the day. He flew for a variety of people, everyone from state troopers to the post office, to other deliveries. Today was clear. Nothing to do but think of Elsie, which was the last thing he wanted to do.

As if on cue, the phone rang.

"Hello?"

"Wyatt, it's Trooper Clements. We have a missing person on a remote island, and seas that are unsuitable for taking the searchers out by boat. Are you available to transport a crew out there?"

There went his clear schedule. Relief rushed into him for a second or two until he finished processing what the trooper had said.

Searchers.

"Just let me know when and where you need me to pick them up." Often he'd have to fly to Homer to pick up people the Troopers needed transported somewhere. It was a short flight, fifteen minutes max, and he didn't mind.

"Thanks. A couple troopers will be in Homer waiting for you. You can get them on your way to the island where the missing person was last seen. The K-9 search team is in your town so they can ride with you to Homer and then to the island."

Which meant Elsie. A day where he was around Elsie,

filled with all the awkward of several nights ago and the continuing concern he had for her.

"Yes, sir."

"She'll meet you at the airport. We told her we'd have transportation waiting for her."

The trooper filled in the rest of the details on coordinates for the island and Wyatt wrote everything down with the pencil that he kept on his small kitchen table for moments like this.

His mind kept pounding Elsie's name as he wrote down details, though. *Elsie. Elsie. Elsie.*

Why was he being thrown back into her path? Did that mean something? He'd wandered from God as a teen but had really been trying to straighten up his life so that he could approach his faith again. Was this some kind of test he had to pass first, to prove that he was above this kind of temptation now? Because Wyatt wasn't sure that he was.

Not that he had any plans to start anything with Elsie. He knew better than that. Just her flirting with him had hit him hard. Reminded him he wasn't the kind of man who deserved her attention, and how she'd only flirted in the first place because she must have thought that was how he communicated. The whole situation had been awkward at best, and he had no idea how to approach any kind of continued interaction with her.

But there wasn't time to worry about that. He had a job to do, and Wyatt was determined not to let people down anymore. Half the time he felt like he was one misstep away from being who he used to be and it terrified him. He couldn't afford mistakes.

This was one more reason why he should ignore Elsie.

It would be so easy to be distracted by her, and he couldn't be distracted by a one-sided crush. Elsie had made it clear years ago he wasn't the kind of man she'd give a second glance to and he didn't think that had changed.

He still wished she'd listened to his concerns, but maybe she was right and the intrusion had been random. Wyatt certainly hoped so.

He ate breakfast quickly, poured coffee into a travel mug and started toward the airport, which wasn't even a mile from his house. That was one of the perks of a town as small as Destruction Point. Besides the houses across the bay, where Elsie lived, nothing in town was far away. Growing up, he'd taken the town for granted, but as an adult he saw how special it was and how lucky he was to call it home.

He worked through his preflight routine, doing his best to keep his focus and not let himself think about the woman he had no business dwelling on. It somewhat worked.

Wyatt wouldn't say he knew the exact moment Elsie arrived at the airport. It wasn't like he could sense her presence or anything so cheesy, but there was a certain… awareness he felt, and when he looked over his shoulder a minute or so later, he saw Elsie.

"I thought I must be imagining things when I walked up here and it was you."

"Because I'm actually working?" He hoped it sounded teasing instead of defensive.

"Because I didn't know you were a pilot. Much less my pilot."

My pilot. Her words shouldn't sink into his heart

like that, shouldn't matter to him the way he was afraid they might.

"My transportation for the day, I mean." She tripped over herself trying to clarify and Wyatt realized this must be awkward for her, too.

"Listen, about the other night…" He blinked, gathering himself. "I pushed you to accept my help. You wanted me to let it go and I didn't. I'm sorry."

She looked uncomfortable for a moment. "About what I said, I didn't mean you were evil or anything…"

"I know."

"It clearly bothered you, and I didn't mean…"

He sighed. "Can we just let it go?"

"If we're going to clear the air, let's really clear it. Or were you just wanting to sweep it under a rug?"

What he was wanting was not to discuss the weirdness of being unintentionally dissed by a woman he thought was beautiful and way too good for him.

"Fine." He inhaled. Exhaled. "Here's the thing, Elsie. I was a different guy in high school. The girls, the flirting incessantly, that's not who I am anymore. Our conversation reminded me of how much I've changed or have tried to change, and I…" He shrugged. "I don't always want to be reminded of the old me. But your judgment of who you remember me to be was fair."

The silence between them stretched, but it was the good kind of stretch. Wyatt waited.

Elsie stuck out her hand. "I said we couldn't start over. But maybe we should as adults. Hi. I'm Elsie Montgomery."

Her easy response made him smile, despite himself. He shook her hand. "Wyatt Chandler."

"Nice to meet you again."

He'd never wanted to be the new him more than he did at this moment.

She'd tried to play it cool, but Elsie's heart had started to pound when she'd seen Wyatt inspecting his plane. Especially when she noticed his broad shoulders and thought of him inside her house, looking tall and intimidating and worried about her.

Touching him, even for a handshake, had been a mistake. She could still feel the sparks on her hand. Inexplicable, but entirely real.

She buried her hand in Willow's fur, trying to rub away the memory of his hand.

"You can wait in the plane if you want. I'm almost done." His smile was relaxed and Elsie was glad they'd had that conversation, awkward as it had been. It wasn't fair that she'd assumed he was the same shallow guy he'd been a decade ago. Not when he was so genuine about wanting to change.

She just hadn't expected to be quite so affected. Of course, he *was* Wyatt Chandler. She'd seen the way he attracted girls like moths to a flame. She'd thought she was…better than that? Past that? That seemed arrogant now.

Add that to her concern that her past might be resurfacing in ways she didn't understand, and Elsie was… several steps past overwhelmed.

She pulled the door open and took in the small plane. It was just big enough for four people, no extra space, but really a nice plane. Elsie didn't know much about airplanes, but she'd ridden in plenty of them, and this was one of the better-kept ones that she'd been in. The last plane that had transported her to a search site had seats covered in duct tape. While she certainly appreciated Alaskans' love for the stuff, it had been a little disconcerting to see so much in an airplane that was supposed to keep her in the sky, even if it was on the seats. She much preferred Wyatt's plane.

She felt jittery. She needed them to get going. To focus fully on her dog and on the task in front of her. Getting called out on a search every few days wasn't unusual at this time of the year. It still felt like it was summer, but the temperatures at night were much less forgiving and the weather less predictable. People made bad choices.

This call sounded like it was on an island not far from the one where she'd been found as a toddler. Did that unnerve her? Yes. Did she think it was connected to the other night?

No.

Probably not?

As Wyatt climbed in, she stole a glance at him. What if she was wrong? She could be putting her life in danger. And his, too? No. She dismissed that thought. Pilots didn't generally hang around during a search. They got paid by the mission, by the flight, and it would be foolish to waste time sitting on the ground when he could be doing other jobs. He'd pick them up that night or the next day if she asked for more time. He would be safe.

At least she didn't have to worry about that.

But as Wyatt started to taxi down the narrow runway, Elsie couldn't help but think that she had plenty of other things to worry about.

FOUR

"You should know," Wyatt said over the headphones when they were airborne and over the ocean that separated Destruction Point from Homer, "that I'm still worried about you."

From the seat beside him, she replied, "What happened to forgetting the other night?"

"Elsie."

Her voice had been too lighthearted. Wyatt was surprised to realize he could read her emotions in her voice well enough to know that she was bothered, too. "What's wrong?"

She frowned at him. "Nothing." Then her shoulders sagged. "I'm not as focused as I'd like to be today. Having someone break into my house bothers me."

"But there's something else, isn't there?" he asked, sensing there was more, while keeping his eyes on the sky ahead and his instruments.

"It's a long story."

"I have time."

"It's a fifteen-minute flight."

She sounded like she wanted to confide in him, like she was talking herself out of it.

She sighed. "Let's just say I'm concerned you might be right."

"That someone is targeting you?"

"Yes, but like I said…concerned. Not certain."

"Then you have no business taking this call. You'll be completely exposed, out in the wilderness."

"That won't make me less safe than I would be at home."

He didn't have an answer to that one. Was she really just as comfortable in the woods as inside her cabin, though? He'd have to say probably yes, judging by the way she'd behaved in the middle of the night.

"What am I supposed to do with this?" Not long until landing. Wyatt didn't have time to sort this out, and as soon as they landed he'd pick up the troopers, whom he was fairly certain Elsie wouldn't want to talk in front of. Did that matter? Or should he force the issue? No, that didn't sit well.

"I don't know. I guess… I just wanted someone to know. Pray or something if you want. That's what your sister would do."

He pushed past the fact that she spoke about prayer in a strange way, like maybe she only half believed in it. "Have you talked to Lindsay about this?"

"I texted to tell her I was fine after I had texted her during the break-in. She was worried. I meant to talk to her on the phone, but never did."

"But you didn't tell her anything about your suspicions or the fact that it might not be random?"

Elsie shook her head.

"Good. Don't."

She frowned.

"If someone's after you, and you keep ignoring it, you're putting people around you in danger, too. I don't want my sister involved in something dangerous."

"I'm not putting anyone at risk on purpose, believe me."

"It's not your fault."

"Sounds like you think it is."

"Wait just a few minutes." Wyatt blew out a breath, went through his pre-landing sequence and brought the plane down on the runway in Homer. He taxied and parked before turning to look at Elsie.

"I'm glad you told me."

"But you said…"

"I just want you to be careful. I think you should keep this close to the vest right now unless you're going to tell law enforcement. I don't want to see any more people hurt or targeted."

He watched as she seemed to internalize his words.

"Do you mind that I told you?"

"Of course not."

Her gaze held his for a moment, then two.

"Okay. Thank you," Elsie said, her voice a little out of breath, and Wyatt felt like he'd maybe passed some sort of unspoken test.

"You're welcome. I have to meet the others. We'll talk later?"

He didn't wait for Elsie to agree, just climbed out of the plane and walked over to where the two troopers, both men, stood. He helped them load their gear—minimal, troopers knew better than to overpack for something like this—into the plane and then they were back in the air, on their way to the coordinates he'd been given.

As they drew closer, he noticed Elsie grow quieter. She'd been chatting with the troopers, about Willow and search and rescue and her recent save of a kid. Wyatt had read about that one in the paper.

Now she seemed uneasy. More so than before.

The ocean beneath them was angry, the waves dark and thick enough to see from the air. They were still half an hour out from the coordinates.

Wyatt glanced over at her. She was pressed to the window, looking down. Was her face paler than it had been a few minutes ago? As the pilot, his job was to get them safely to their destination, but he also felt responsible for his passengers' well-being in general. Or that was what he told himself.

"You all right?"

She turned to him. Nodded. He wasn't imagining things. She looked clammy.

"Are you sure—"

"Wyatt, please." Her voice was pleading and he nodded once, then forced himself to focus his attention on the plane. Compartmentalize.

The two law enforcement officers in the rear seats continued to chat with each other, but Wyatt paid little attention. When it was finally time to land, it required all his focus to the point that he could no longer worry about Elsie or anything else. The sea was choppier than he preferred for water landings, but it was nothing outside his skill level. Easing the plane down, he made a fairly smooth landing and then brought the plane as close to the island as possible.

He managed to beach the plane on the shore in such a way that his passengers should be able to climb out the door, walk down the float and step directly onto sand instead of wading through water. He'd noticed that like any practical Alaskan, Elsie was wearing Xtratuf boots, brown fishing boots that came high up the calf and were all-purpose wear up here. She'd be fine even if she had to step in a little bit of water.

They all scrabbled out, and he stood by the plane and watched as the troopers briefed her on the situation. Elsie still looked unsettled, but he believed in her ability to find the missing person. It was clear that Elsie's dog was special. Hopefully they would be able to find whoever it was. Elsie could take care of them, he was sure of it.

But who was going to take care of Elsie?

The question sneaked in uninvited, but he still wondered at the answer.

When the troopers walked higher on the shore and she turned to look at him, he motioned her closer.

"What do you need?" she asked, looking up at him in a way that made him wish he were a better man.

"Are you sure you're okay?" he asked.

She shook her head. "Why?"

"Your face…your expression…"

"Oh." She looked away. "It's just this place."

"Not a fan of remote islands?"

"Not ones around here."

She met his eyes again, held his gaze and shook her head slowly. As she did, understanding started to dawn, and Wyatt felt his stomach waver uneasily.

"It was an island not far from here where I was left as a kid."

"As a kid?"

"A three-year-old." She swallowed hard and Wyatt thought her eyes might be shining with unshed tears.

He couldn't imagine being alone at three, even inside a house. But here? In the untamed Alaskan wilderness that had claimed more than one adult life?

It was hard not to imagine a three-year-old version of Elsie, alone, scared.

"And there happens to be a missing person here now?" He raised his eyebrows.

"I know." Elsie shook her head. "When I knew where we were heading, I wondered."

"What if it's a trap?"

"What if it's not? I can't leave someone here. Lost people need to be found, Wyatt. Someone has to do it."

Couldn't someone else, though? As though she heard his thoughts, Elsie shook her head. And he understood— no one else around did K-9 search and rescue, and in rugged terrain like this, having a dog to help search was a huge advantage.

Still, anxiety wouldn't release its grip on him. "Let me help you. Please."

She seemed to be considering him. Studying him. What did she see?

"Okay."

Okay?

"I could use another searcher. Willow is the star of the show here. I read her cues and help her know what areas to search. I could use someone else with me. It's better to be in pairs and those guys were just telling me that they had planned to stay together. If we split up, we will be more efficient, but I'm not eager to be alone here."

Honest. Vulnerable.

"Whatever you need. I want to help."

"Thank you."

Any man who could listen to her insist she didn't need his help and then graciously offer it when it became apparent that she did need it couldn't be too bad.

Elsie reached down and petted Willow, took a deep breath. She was distracted today, too in her own head and her own past to go through the motions like she usually did. She felt out of the cone, and not sure how to get herself mentally back to where she wanted to be.

Desperate, she closed her eyes, took a couple of breaths and tried to let them out slowly.

Nothing to do now but focus on what needed to be done. The thought of someone dying because she had been distracted was unacceptable to her. They were counting on her to find them.

She wondered if the troopers would have asked for her and Willow's help if they'd known that this was so close to the island where she'd been abandoned as a kid.

Who had abandoned her was still a major question. Foul play had to have been involved somewhere, especially in the absence of a missing-person report that could have shed light on her identity. But it all remained a mystery.

"Ready?" she made herself turn to Willow and ask, desperate to move past this.

Willow looked up at her, ice blue eyes focused.

"That's my girl," Elsie said with a smile and a small laugh. There was something reassuring in knowing that Willow was ready to work, even if her handler was struggling today. She had to do her best for the dog. It was amazing to Elsie how when people and dogs worked together, the humans were usually the weak link. The dogs knew what they were doing and did their jobs well.

She gave Willow the command to search and the dog ran ahead of her, though Elsie knew she wouldn't go far. She and Wyatt would trail, waiting and hoping for Willow to pick up a scent.

"How will she know who to search for?"

"She won't this time," Elsie answered as they moved onto higher ground, trading the dark gray rocks of the coastal beach for the larger rocks and grassy area that made up the higher part of the shore. Willow had already headed into the woods, and they followed her. "I gave her instructions to search for any humans at all, since as far as we know, the four of us and whoever's missing are the only people on this island."

"Won't she just find the troopers?"

Elsie shrugged. "She may. But without a strong scent item from the missing person, this is the best option."

"They didn't have anything for you?"

Elsie shook her head. "No." She hadn't been told much about the person they were searching for, which wasn't her preference. While the dog was the strongest member of any K-9 search and rescue team, Elsie was also a valuable member. Her human brain could synthesize information that Willow's couldn't, and Elsie took pride in the number of trainings she'd attended. She always wanted to learn and work better.

Without more information on the victim, she couldn't make a very good profile to help her search more intelligently. She'd have to talk to the troopers later and get more information. For now, she just knew the missing person was a female in her midtwenties. She and a friend had come to the island to hike and became separated. Only the friend had made it back to town and had reported the other woman missing. There would be a record of her name and presence on the island, at least, even if the friend hadn't made it back. Because of its remote location and the fact that it was owned by the forest service, they kept a log of all visitors.

It was an isolated place to hike, but Elsie knew that Midnight Ridge, the mountain that made up the high point of the island, was a destination for some hikers who wanted an incredible view.

They and the missing woman should be the only ones here. At least legally. They continued through the woods, Elsie watching the ground under her feet, the thick trees around her, for any sign that someone else had been here recently.

"So what made you want to work with search dogs?" Wyatt asked, apparently trying to start a conversation.

"I'm a little busy right now. No time for that." Elsie blew out a breath of frustration. Didn't he realize she was working?

"So what do you do right now? I thought you just followed Willow."

He got points for remembering her dog's name, she would give him that.

"I'm observing, trying to see evidence someone may have left behind. Watching Willow's behavior… She has an alert bark when she's found what she's looking for, and I like to pay attention to her overall attitude and see what I can read from that."

"Like what?"

It was harder for her to explain than she would have thought, and for a moment Elsie almost wished she were alone. Then she remembered that she had been alone on an island like this once, and that someone might be after her now.

Willow was following some kind of scent trail, made by either a hiker or game, rather than just blazing through the woods. That implied to Elsie that their missing hiker may have come this way.

She needed to ask the troopers for more information about the missing woman if the search lasted longer than today, which her gut was telling her would be the case.

Willow's ears perked suddenly, and Elsie's vision tunneled in on the dog. Willow looked to the left, ran off at a sprint.

"She's got something!" Elsie tossed the explanation behind her and took off at a run behind her dog, not looking back to see if Wyatt followed. The job took first priority, and she couldn't afford to ask Willow to slow down. Any number of things, even a shift in the wind, could make the dog lose the trail.

They hadn't been hiking for long. The chances of the missing person being this close to the edge of the woods didn't seem likely to Elsie, but she could be wrong. Willow had probably caught a heavy patch of scent, and it would still take some determination and patience to reach where the missing person actually was.

Willow stopped. Elsie stopped, too, then crept slowly toward the dog.

A low growl echoed from Willow's throat.

Elsie's heartbeat caught in her chest. This shouldn't be happening. Willow was trained to find people, and search dogs typically displayed enthusiasm and joy when they'd succeeded. Chills chased down Elsie's spine.

She looked back.

No Wyatt. She slowed her breathing to try to fight back the panic. Surely he couldn't be far behind her.

Willow was one of the only constants in her life. A source of reassurance. But as much as Willow usually made Elsie feel better, the dog's reaction was scaring her now.

She and Willow were not alone here. Someone was close.

And not, Elsie thought, the person they'd been searching for.

"Willow, no," Elsie whispered to the dog, who paused her growling but continued to stare into the woods, looking like she was ready to defend them both.

Elsie ran through the list of things that could make her act this way. Animal? Possibly a moose or bear. But Willow had insisted they come this way, which implied that she'd caught the scent of...

Anyone. She'd asked her to search for people.

The searchers and the missing woman were *not* the only people on this island, Elsie was confident of it.

"I told you to stop hiding. You can't run from the past forever."

The voice from the other night. Her past... A gunshot split the air.

Elsie's head jerked to the right. "Willow, come!"

The dog sprang toward her, and together they took off at a sprint, back the way they'd come.

She should have told Wyatt about the voice.

It was a strange thing to think about as she sprinted through the woods, mindful of the roots that tangled in the soil underfoot, trying to make sure she stayed upright. But she should have trusted him more.

She shouldn't have gotten herself into this situation. How many times had she been frustrated by the willful ignorance of some people? People skied in avalanche conditions, likely telling themselves they were safe, and had to be rescued or, worse, recovered by search teams.

And now she'd done the same thing. Whoever had been in her cabin a few nights ago *was* after her. She'd been foolish to ignore the obvious threat.

Wyatt had been right.

Imagine, Wyatt being more responsible than Elsie was. How the world had changed.

She owed him an apology, if she made it back safely.

That and the whole truth.

FIVE

One moment. That was all the time it had taken for Wyatt to completely lose Elsie. She'd taken off after the dog and he'd caught his foot on a root and gone down.

He stood up fast, but she'd already been out of his sight, maybe not entirely surprising in woods this thick. He could almost feel them pressing in on him, memories from that night, of knowing someone was inside Elsie's house twining with his own imaginings of what it might have been like for Elsie to be abandoned here as a kid. There was no avoiding it—he was panicking at this point. That was the honest truth.

Hopefully for nothing. Search and rescue was her job. She did this all the time, but that didn't erase his desire to protect her. Maybe because she'd always seemed fragile to him, with something in her eyes that was a little vulnerable. Maybe because in high school she hadn't dated much and he'd always been under the impression that there was something in her that needed shielding.

Those impressions conflicted with the capable woman he'd talked to the other night, the one who didn't seem fazed by hiking through the woods in the middle of the night, or terrified by a home intruder.

Still, Wyatt told himself now, he didn't like the fact that he'd lost her in the woods. Or she'd lost him.

Probably she was fine. Probably he was losing his head for nothing.

The first gunshot convinced him he was wrong.

He started running, willing himself to see something, anything that would indicate which way Elsie and Willow had gone. There was a barely discernible trail they'd been following—had they stayed on it?

Against all his rising panic, he made himself stop. Listen.

Something off to the left. Running feet or just the wind in the branches?

He didn't know.

He wondered if he should call for her. It could alert her to his presence, or call an attacker's attention to her and put her in more danger.

Or would the shooter back off if they knew they weren't alone?

It was worth the risk. "Elsie!" he yelled as he ran toward the noise. "Elsie!"

A blur caught his eye seconds before he felt the impact of Elsie's petite body colliding with his.

He caught her upper arms. "Hey, it's okay."

Her eyes were wide and she shook her head. "No. It's not. Run." And she was off again, backtracking toward the shore, Willow running along right beside her.

At least he was sure the dog wasn't going to let harm come to Elsie if she could help it, but Willow wouldn't be able to stop a bullet from hitting her handler.

Wyatt positioned himself behind both of them as they

ran. The blur of trees made him dizzy but he stayed focused ahead of him.

Then the woods opened up. Beach. Open air.

Elsie and Willow were up and into the plane before Wyatt could catch up.

"You don't think he'll follow you all the way here?" he asked when he'd climbed inside to the pilot's seat.

"I have no idea."

He radioed the troopers who were on the island searching, explained the situation.

Mostly.

As Wyatt talked to them on the radio, he watched Elsie's eyes widen. She still clearly wasn't a fan of looping law enforcement in to what was going on. He supposed if they knew of the danger, they might take her off the case, but he didn't think this case was worth her life.

He clicked the radio volume down when he'd finished his conversation, scanned the beach and, satisfied there was no sign of whoever had been in the woods, turned to face Elsie, who was holding Willow in her lap, stroking her.

A fifty-something-pound husky made a strange lapdog, but he wasn't about to say so.

"Thank you for not telling them it might be a specific threat against me," she said immediately, leaving him no time to wonder how to broach the subject with her.

He nodded, feeling the heaviness of the situation settle on him. "Mind telling me why you're so determined for them not to find out? They're the good guys, you know. They could help you."

Something in her eyes flickered.

"I don't want my personal business becoming common knowledge. I don't want to walk back into the past." She turned away from him, her eyes on some far-off point.

"Sometimes you have to face things and not run from them."

Elsie flicked her gaze back to him, her eyes burning into him. "You have *no* idea what you're talking about. *No* idea what this would mean for me."

"Because you won't tell me." He spit the words without thinking, then took a deep breath. He was being insensitive, and she was right—he didn't have any idea why she was so upset.

"Listen," he tried again, "a woman is in danger. A woman who could be tied to you."

"She's a random hiker. The fact that she is on the island has to be a coincidence, Wyatt. I don't think anyone brought her here as some kind of bait for me. Not when they could just try to abduct me from my house again."

"Maybe they decided that wouldn't work after the other night."

"I have no idea. But if there's even a suspicion on the troopers' part that I'm connected, I'll be taken off the case," she said in a soft voice. "We can't be taken off this case. Willow is the best. Time is of the essence in any search and rescue case, and frankly, we know the terrain in this part of the state better than anyone. There's not another K-9 search and rescue team that I'm aware of for at least a hundred miles. I can't let people stay lost."

He heard her desperation and wondered if she realized the words she left unsaid, that she knew what it was like to be lost and without much of a hope of rescue.

He felt that way sometimes about his faith. There was a verse about that somewhere in the Bible, about being lost and without hope. He'd certainly felt that way once.

"Why do you focus so much on that, wanting people to not stay lost?" he finally found the courage to ask. He didn't have the right to expect an answer, but he found himself hoping that she would stop holding him at arm's length.

Eyes wide, she was almost looking at him like he'd lost his marbles for asking.

"Okay, yes, obviously you don't want them to stay lost because you're a good person," he clarified, "but it seems to mean even more to you. Is it because of the fact that you were…"

"Lost?" She said it without hesitation, even though the word applied to Elsie made Wyatt flinch.

"Yeah."

She rubbed her forehead. "Yes, probably. I know what it's like to be lost, to wonder if anyone is going to find you, see you, if you even matter enough for people to search for."

He could still read the guardedness in her eyes, and Wyatt knew when not to push.

"I hate that you went through that," Wyatt said, though it seemed inadequate.

Another few beats of silence.

"Thank you for not apologizing for it. I hate it when people do that." She looked away and Wyatt knew that was all she had in her to share emotionally at the moment.

Thank You that she trusted me. He whispered a quick prayer in his heart.

"I have to find her," she reiterated, jaw set.

"Listen, I hear you," he said, "but your safety…" He wished he could reach out to her, touch her arm, her shoulder, just something to convey that he wanted her to be okay, to keep her safe. But she wasn't his to touch. She'd shy away from him, and that was the last thing he wanted, especially when it seemed like she was starting to trust him, however slightly.

"My safety is going to be in jeopardy no matter where I am. It does seem like they're after me specifically. He called my name. When he said he'd been searching for me the other night, I—"

Panic rising in his throat, Wyatt cut her off. "What?"

She didn't answer.

"You let me think there was a *chance* this was random, though that was hard to swallow, when all along you knew that whoever broke into your house specifically knew who you were?"

Elsie looked out the window to her right, avoiding eye contact.

She'd proved just over the last few hours that she was extremely smart, reading Willow's silent cues in a way that had amazed him. So how could she be so careless with her own safety? She was heroic, sure, but did she view her life as worth so little?

"You're worth keeping safe, too. You know that, right?" he asked.

The question took her off guard enough that she turned and looked at him, a frown scrunching her eyebrows together. "What are you talking about?"

"You act like only other people matter. That you're just…possible collateral damage if something happens to you when you're on a search. You matter more than that."

"I would never intentionally step into a situation with too much risk, Wyatt. They teach us in search and rescue training." Now her voice had an edge to it, a bite he wouldn't have thought her capable of. He was seeing a new side to Elsie. She was small, quiet. But she wasn't a pushover, he was seeing now.

"Maybe not, but you're putting yourself at risk now and you just don't seem concerned." His frustration escalated and he contracted his muscles and released the tension, trying to let go of the physical effects of being upset. At home he'd take Sven for a run or do push-ups if something upset him this much, though he couldn't remember the last time something had.

"I'm not... I'm not trying to do that." She was frustrated, too. He could hear it in her tone. When she finally shifted in her seat to fully look at him, he could see the hurt in her eyes.

Talk to me. He met her gaze. Stayed still.

"I'm not used to anyone caring," she finally said, looking down. A stray lock of hair fell into her face.

Without thinking, Wyatt reached forward and pushed it back, and as he did so, Elsie lifted her head again. He realized how close they were now, their faces closer than they'd ever been. Twelve inches? Ten?

He could kiss her.

The thought came from out of nowhere, but his eyes dropped to her lips and then he glanced back up.

Something shifted in her gaze. She'd seen him consider it. She wasn't backing away.

Kissing her wasn't what was best for her right now.

For either of them. She didn't need to know that she mattered in the context of a romantic relationship. She needed to know that she *mattered*. Full stop. A kiss could weaken that message, one he wanted her to hear. Elsie mattered to him too much to kiss right now, strange as that thought was.

"I care," he whispered.

She blinked, almost like she was absorbing the message, letting it soak into her. Believing it?

When she finally looked away, he felt bereft. But also strangely hopeful. She hadn't argued with him, hadn't flinched at his admission that he cared about her.

Elsie had gotten under his skin. He didn't know what to think about it. Wasn't sure he liked it.

It would be easy to wonder why he'd volunteered to help. He didn't need this kind of frustration in his life, not when he was trying to start over, live better. Stay peaceful and boring and all of that, like he felt a good Christian maybe should. Heaven knew, quite literally, that he'd had enough excitement in his teens and twenties to last a lifetime. Flying was enough of an adrenaline rush. He should be pursuing other things in his life that kept him calm. Steady.

Right? He'd been a different man for five years now, but was five years really enough time to trust that he'd actually changed? Wyatt didn't want to risk it, didn't want to turn back into who he'd been before.

He *had* to keep playing it safe.

The mental picture of his sweater-vest-wearing pastor father, prepping for a sermon late at night in his armchair, came to mind.

Yes. That should be Wyatt's goal. So certainly someone like Elsie who made his blood pressure skyrocket like this could only spell disaster for him. She brought color to his life. Feeling.

Maybe he couldn't be trusted with feelings and color.

Maybe he shouldn't have gotten involved.

Except then who would try to protect her? Fight for her even against herself?

This situation was hard for him to handle. He didn't know how to do this.

But he'd sure rather be in this mess himself right now than be left with the knowledge that he'd abandoned her to face it alone.

From her seat, Elsie watched the play of emotions across Wyatt's face, tried to read him like she'd read a K-9, though in her experience people were substantially harder to understand than dogs, even if she'd had extensive psychology training and education.

He was upset, she understood that part even without her degrees, but she wasn't sure why he seemed angry.

Interestingly, she didn't feel threatened by his anger. Something in the back of her mind usually recoiled at the emotion in general—she rarely got angry herself, as it just didn't seem safe.

When she thought it, there was that dark place again, where she'd pictured her toddler self earlier. A cave? A closet?

People were yelling. *That* anger didn't feel safe.

She swallowed hard, pulled herself out of the flashback before it could continue.

Wyatt's expression wavered. His brows knit together. "What? What's wrong now?"

Could he read her mind? More than once she'd been told she didn't wear her emotions on her face, so what was with Wyatt's almost uncanny ability to understand them?

"Nothing." She shook her head, like that would make it true. Her earlier determination to be more honest with Wyatt felt like a two-by-four to the face. "I mean, something. A weird memory, sorry, random." Elsie blew out a breath. "The man in the woods knew my name." She restated it, trying to ground herself back in the present, process what was facing her *right now*, not what she'd faced in the past.

"But you don't want to be taken off this case."

"If the missing woman died, I'd never forgive myself."

She saw the tightening of his jawline and reached over and laid a hand on his arm. "Hey, I hear what you're saying. But there's got to be a way for me to not back out of this and still stay reasonably safe."

She was proud of herself for getting the words out, because she hadn't counted on the distraction Wyatt's arm would be under her hand. He was wearing a fleece, the perfect layering tool for this kind of wet, chilly weather, so it wasn't as though her hand was even touching skin, but…

It was still enough to make it hard to focus on her thoughts. Still enough to make her hearken back to the ridiculous crush she'd had on him in high school, especially when coupled with that strange moment they'd just shared. She'd really thought he'd been about to kiss her. More than once she'd let her guard down with him, even though she didn't do that with people, ever. And it hadn't been as scary as she'd anticipated. What did that even mean? Elsie looked away, moved her hand slowly so it wouldn't look as though touching him had affected her.

"Maybe." He sounded doubtful, and if she wasn't imagining things, there was something in his eyes that hadn't been there a few moments ago.

Maybe she wasn't the only one affected. Would that be good or bad?

In light of everything happening, almost certainly bad. Elsie couldn't afford a distraction right now. Neither her personal nor professional life could.

Wyatt Chandler, six feet of gorgeous who would say something like *I care* to her and give every evidence of meaning it? He was a distraction.

Movement outside the plane caught her eye and her heart skipped. She nearly ducked for cover in case it was her would-be attacker, when she saw it was the two state troopers emerging from the woods at a jog. Responding to Wyatt's radio call, she guessed.

Wyatt eased the door of the plane open and stepped out. Elsie followed, unwilling to let someone fight her battles for her, not even one that should be fairly easy, like explaining to the troopers that they'd heard a gunshot and threats uttered in the woods, while still leaving out details that made it clear she'd been targeted.

Okay, so not that easy of a battle. Maybe she was thankful to have someone on her side.

"Everything okay?" Trooper Holland asked, his gaze swinging from Elsie to Wyatt.

"Fine," Elsie answered, deciding she should be the one to talk. "It appears there's a bad actor somewhere in the woods. We heard a gun and a male voice. He said something threatening to me."

The troopers exchanged a concerned look. Holland said, "What did he say?"

"It's a bit of a jumble." She made herself hold the man's gaze so he didn't sense she was hiding anything. And it was true—she didn't remember the *exact* words…just the sentiment. Close enough. But technically not a lie. "Just something threatening. I didn't stop to think about it. He started shooting, and we ran."

Her heart pounded faster, but she was sure she was doing the right thing. Wyatt was willing to help her, after all. They could work together to find the missing woman and then worry about why someone was after her. If someone died because the troopers thought she was too close to the situation, she didn't know how she'd ever move past that.

"Could you show us where the shots were fired? It's an outside chance, but if we could find the casings, it could be useful evidence."

Wyatt was looking at Elsie for guidance. Surprise and appreciation made her hold back a smile. He was a skilled pilot and Alaskan outdoorsman. He could answer their question, but he was looking to her to see what she said.

She nodded at the troopers. "I could lead you back there."

"You're sure?" Wyatt asked her, then looked at the troopers. "Is it safe enough?" His voice once again betrayed his genuine concern for her safety.

"It doesn't seem reasonable that the person could be sitting there waiting," Trooper Holland explained.

"If we approach and it's not safe to investigate, we'll come back."

Anxiety weighing heavier with each step, Elsie led them back through the woods. Earlier she'd been focused only on the job at hand, but now as they moved with stealth, she was taking in more of her surroundings. She wondered how similar these surroundings were to the island where she'd been found. Extremely so, from what she could remember. It wasn't difficult to picture herself as a small child, hiding in the woods so much like these. She remembered being lost, remembered the nights she'd spent alone on that island, how scared the dark had made her...

Why couldn't she remember what came before that? Her flashback in the plane had gone into more detail than she remembered ever feeling or imagining before. The darkness and sense of discomfort, fear—that was familiar to her. But the yelling she could now remember hearing? That was new. What else would she remember if she let herself? And were these memories finally resurfacing because of the island?

All her life, through family tree school projects and health history forms, Elsie had thought she'd wanted to know who she was, where she'd come from.

What happened if those answers weren't what she wanted them to be? Did she still want to know?

A rustle in the branches stopped her short, caught her breath.

Wyatt's voice was low and steady in her ears. "Just a bird. You're doing okay."

It shouldn't have calmed her as much as it did, but

she felt the tension leave her shoulders and she took a long breath in and out.

Elsie sensed the tension in Willow as they approached the location where the shots had been fired. She had taken the dog's vest off to let Willow know they weren't searching anymore officially, but her natural instincts still had her smelling the air for lingering scent. She clearly didn't understand why they'd be returning to an unsafe place.

"Around here," she finally said when they'd reached the spot. "I heard him talk somewhere over there." She motioned. "And then he started shooting." Chills threatened again, and she rubbed her arms almost without realizing it.

Trooper Holland seemed to notice her discomfort. With a glance at his partner, he spoke up. "This isn't conventional, but maybe the two of you should head back to the cover of the plane."

His partner nodded in agreement.

Clearly they were unwilling to expose them to danger longer than necessary, which Elsie appreciated, even if she did dislike being coddled as a rule.

The cold, damp air of the island was chilling her all the way to the inside, and much to her shame, Elsie knew that if the troopers or Wyatt insisted she stop searching, she would be tempted to listen. But she knew equally that she couldn't do that, not and live with herself.

"I understand why it's not safe for us to stick around here, but I do need to keep searching somewhere on the island," Elsie made herself say, her shoulders as squared as she could make them, though she couldn't say if that physical show of confidence was to convince the troopers or herself.

She felt Wyatt's gaze on her and could only guess at his emotions. Fighting to keep her breathing steady, she waited to hear what the troopers would say. Technically they'd contracted her services. They could decide to call off the search if they deemed it unsafe.

"Let's hold off until tomorrow," one of them finally said, then looked to Wyatt. "If you could get the K-9 team back home, then come back for us, we should know more then."

Blinking back tears, determined not to let them show and risk coming across as unprofessional, Elsie nodded. She never cried, almost never. But this place seemed to lay her bare emotionally.

Neither she nor Wyatt said anything as they walked back toward the plane. The woods here didn't feel like comfort to Elsie. They felt empty, like the emptiness was a tangible thing. There was too much to consider, too many things from her past and present confusing Elsie, for her to make any sense of her mind right now.

"You okay?" Wyatt asked as they emerged from the woods back onto the rocky shoreline.

How to even answer that? Elsie shook her head.

"How can I help?"

"You've done enough, really. I appreciated you being out there today."

"What if I did it again? Whenever they let you come back and search. Tomorrow. If there's a day you're working there after that. If there's another case after this and the threat against you still hasn't been dealt with."

He was offering more than she could imagine, someone to watch her back while she watched her dog's, to be her voice when she was busy being Willow's.

"I don't think I can ask that of you." She'd vowed to be more honest with him, and this level of honesty was almost brutal. She'd thought it was just the island that made her feel defenseless and vulnerable, but maybe Wyatt was part of it, too. She rarely looked so deeply and truly at herself, her motivations or the goings-on around her with the same level of black-and-white clarity that Wyatt seemed to.

"You're not asking. I'm offering."

His eyes met hers.

Dark, warm eyes. A brown that reminded her of the Alaskan woods in the best way. What if she said yes to him and she couldn't protect her heart? He was a man with broad shoulders, kind eyes and an easy laugh who seemed bound and determined to keep her safe. She *knew* better than to fall for a guy like Wyatt, even if he had supposedly reformed.

What if she said no to him and it cost her her life? Someone else their life?

Elsie held her breath. Closed her eyes. Waited to know what to say. And wished for a second that she had someone else to ask for help. Lindsay would pray at a time like this. Elsie wondered what it would be like to have that kind of support, what it would be like to finally not be so alone.

SIX

"Yes." The word left Elsie's mouth like a whisper and Wyatt could breathe again, releasing the breath he hadn't realized he'd been holding.

"Good." He readied the plane for takeoff, not sure what else there was to say.

The flight back to Destruction Point was quiet. He had questions for her, but with his earlier frustration and fear at the danger facing her in mind, he waited till he'd landed safely. Then he turned to her before she exited the plane. He almost reached for her, but after the shock that had gone through his body at her simple touch earlier, he wasn't willing to play with that kind of fire again. Besides the obvious reasons—like the fact that she deserved a man who'd always been decent and hadn't just started to turn his life around recently—he also wanted to focus on keeping her safe right now. He couldn't afford any other feelings.

"You said that the intruder the first night said something."

Her eyes got that guarded look again, like a shield had gone up.

"Would you tell me what they said?"

She didn't answer him, though a look of fear crossed her face. She opened the airplane door and climbed out, her dog following behind her. Wyatt made himself stay quiet. He was learning that pushing Elsie was a surefire way to meet resistance. It would be much better to wait.

"I don't remember exactly."

"Like you didn't remember today?"

She raised an eyebrow at him as a slow smile inched across her tense facial features. "You caught that, huh?"

"It didn't take a rocket scientist. They were just distracted."

"As long as it worked," Elsie said with a shrug, then blew out a breath. "The other night, the man in my house told me to stop hiding and that he was going to find me. Or that he was always going to find me? Something like that." She mumbled the last sentence, but Wyatt heard enough clearly. "And he mentioned 'the past' in this vague kind of way."

"Your past?" he asked.

She didn't look at him, didn't answer. It was more than answer enough.

This was not random. There was no way it could have been.

Who *was* he? Who was trying to find her?

And what did he mean by find her? He wondered if she was hiding from someone intentionally.

He looked at her but Elsie was already shaking her head. "Before you ask, I don't know. I don't know any of the answers to what you're wondering."

"You have to know more than I do."

Hesitation.

"Not really."

Why did he feel like every layer he finally got behind just left more layers in its place? Elsie Montgomery was far more of a mystery than he'd have ever guessed.

"Let me take you home?" Wyatt cleared his throat. "To your house." A head shake. "I want to make sure you're safe."

This time she didn't appear to be hiding any emotions and he saw understanding in her smile. "Thanks. And yes, I think that would be wise. Just in case anything happened at my cabin while I was gone…"

He understood. Two of them could more effectively sweep the place for intruders. She had really meant it earlier when she'd told him he could help. He'd heard her reply, had felt relief at it, but wasn't sure he'd really expected her to follow through to this degree.

They walked to the docks.

"Your boat or mine?" Elsie asked, looking up at him with clear eyes.

Wyatt took a deep breath. "You'd better drive yours and I'll drive mine. That way you're not left without transportation once I head back out."

"Smart." She was frowning. "I should have thought of that."

"Don't be so hard on yourself."

Her raised eyebrows seemed to point out the irony of his instruction. That was different, Wyatt knew, even if Elsie didn't. It was one thing to be a perfectionist like Elsie seemed to be, demanding something from herself that was asking too much. He wasn't a perfectionist, not even close. If he was hard on himself, he *deserved* it.

They walked first to Elsie's boat, which Willow jumped

into with the ease of a dog who had grown up around the water and was used to using boats as transportation.

Come to think of it, she'd been amazing on the plane, too.

"That's quite the dog you've got, you know? I love my dog, but Sven took a lot longer to adjust to the plane than that, and boats still scare him. He just presses down into the deck the entire ride. And when he has to climb in one, he sort of slinks toward it like 'here we go again.'"

Elsie laughed. "She's a great dog, but it's training, too. We worked on those things when she was a puppy, because they're necessary in a dog that does search and rescue work. We can't worry about how she's going to respond in situations like that. She needs to be all but bombproof."

"That's a lot of training. Says a lot about the quality of her trainer."

Elsie blushed. "I mean, like you said, she's a good dog."

He let that one go. Clearly she didn't want to take the compliment, but she did deserve it.

After looking around to satisfy himself with the knowledge that her boat hadn't been tampered with, Wyatt headed to his own boat and prepped it for the ride across the bay. Had it really only been a few days ago he'd done this same trip in the middle of the night? Such a short time had passed since then, but it felt like so much had changed. Elsie had gone from a near stranger, just a friend of his sister's, to someone he cared about, as a friend, in such a short time.

Or was it that short? They'd known each other almost their whole lives.

No, it was still short because Wyatt had spent so

much of his life self-absorbed and barely noticing his sister's mousy friend. Who was not as mousy or timid as he'd initially believed.

She still needed protection, though. The danger against her was like a living thing, growing as time passed and becoming clearer and clearer.

It bothered Wyatt that someone had spoken to her during both incidents. Bold criminals seemed to be the more dangerous type, just from what he'd observed while flying for the troopers and watching them do what they did.

The ride across the bay passed quickly and soon Wyatt was beaching the boat, downing the anchor and walking toward Elsie's cabin. It looked undisturbed, but appearances didn't always tell the whole story.

Elsie herself came to mind again. He was too intrigued by her. He needed to stay focused on the goal, which was keeping her safe. Then he'd be back out of her life, back in his own somewhat empty one, just existing…

Yeah, it didn't sound good that way.

But that was just the way it had to be. Wyatt should know better by now than to want something he couldn't have.

He made his way toward her cabin, struck by some of the similarities this little corner of Alaska had to the island where they'd been today. The trees were the same tall Sitka spruce, the ground damp from ocean air and humidity, moss everywhere.

Did Elsie notice the similarities? The island seemed to scare her and make her go into some dark place in her head where he couldn't reach her. This place seemed to make her comfortable.

No sooner had Wyatt processed through the thought than he wondered if it was true. She was comfortable here, but was she happy? She certainly seemed to enjoy the independence, but she was so isolated. By choice? A weird tie to her past?

Not his business, really.

"Everything looks okay from here." Elsie spoke up beside him. He hadn't even seen her walk over from where she'd tied up her boat at her small dock. He needed to be more situationally aware as long as they were involved in whatever kind of investigation this was.

"That's good."

Conversation was awkward, like they'd been through too much too quickly but that was outside of town, outside of places that made up their normal life. Now it felt like they were almost starting over.

"Ready to go check it out? You still don't mind? You don't have to." Her words were almost shy.

"I want to help."

"Why? Why are you helping me so much? Yeah, we both know your sister, but we barely know each other." The urgency in her tone wasn't demanding, just curious. Wondering.

Did he even have an answer? Wyatt himself wasn't sure.

"Maybe..." He trailed off. "Maybe it doesn't make a lot of sense. To me, either, to be honest, but I wanted to help the other night and now it's even more important to me to keep you out of danger."

"Why?"

"Because I..." *Care about her?* He did, but the words

would sound empty, especially coming from him, or would sound like a flirtation he didn't mean.

Instead he didn't say anything, just shook his head. "It's just important, that's all."

That seemed to be enough for Elsie. She nodded once, and they walked to her cabin. As she reached to open the door, Wyatt took a fortifying breath. The way danger seemed to be growing, his self-imposed task of keeping her safe seemed to be getting more and more difficult.

He could only hope—maybe even pray—that he would be able to protect her.

Elsie was confident in the search she and Wyatt had done of her cabin hours before, but that wasn't making sleeping any easier. She couldn't even seem to find comfort in the fact that Willow had gone to sleep peacefully, giving no indication that anything was out of place.

Every settling noise that the cabin made, every call of an owl from outside her window, all of it heightened her senses and put her on edge. It had been all she could do to convince Wyatt not to sleep on his boat, which she'd discovered had been his initial plan.

She and Wyatt searched the cabin, and then she'd made them each a cup of coffee. They'd sat in relative silence while they drank their coffee, which she'd appreciated. It was rare to find another person who didn't mind some silence, but Elsie needed it in her life, for reasons she couldn't quite explain. When coffee was finished, he'd told her good-night and left.

It wasn't until later that she'd realized she'd never heard his boat. Unease swirling in her stomach, worry for him and his safety rising in her, she'd walked with Willow down to the beach, vigilant the entire way for anyone who might be lurking among the spruce trees. She'd found no one with ill intentions, just Wyatt's boat right where it had been earlier.

"I thought you were leaving," she'd called from the beach.

"What if I just sleep on my boat?"

Sweet man. It was the first thing that came to mind and the thought startled Elsie, though she knew it wasn't a bad description for him. "I'm fine, Wyatt. Go home."

It had taken a little more convincing, but eventually he'd pulled up his anchor and headed back into town, and Elsie had gone back into her quiet cabin.

That he'd been willing to sleep in a too-small area on a too-small-to-be-comfortable-to-sleep-on boat in the open to keep her safe meant a lot. She wasn't used to anyone taking care of her. Oh, her foster parents had been fine, no neglect or anything. But she hadn't felt... *cared* for. Not in the way other kids seemed to. She'd always felt just a bit like she was on her own, even as a very young child.

Now Wyatt was making that untrue. She wasn't facing this danger alone.

It couldn't mean too much to her. She couldn't let it. Being in close proximity to Wyatt so often was bound to resurrect the ridiculous crush she'd had in high school, which was all the more dangerous since he seemed to have changed. Did people change, *really*, though? Or would she be a fool to ignore his past?

Elsie was confident she knew the answers to those questions, whether she liked them or not, which meant she was going to have to do a better job of keeping some defenses up, not letting him get too close.

So she'd sent him home and she was alone in her cabin with her dog, her mind replaying the night of the break-in and the encounter in the woods on repeat.

Maybe she should just give up on sleep and have another cup of coffee and read. At least then that way danger wouldn't catch her unprepared. Would that really be better, though?

She needed to sleep. Elsie took a long breath in, thought of her dog and the way Willow trusted her when it was time to rest. She needed that, too, to be able to trust that it was safe to sleep.

Again, she thought of Lindsay, whom she'd texted earlier with only vague descriptions of the trouble she'd been in. Lindsay was going through her own stressful time at work; it wasn't fair to burden her too much. Besides, she still felt funny admitting that she was hanging out with her friend's older brother.

And enjoying it more than she would have expected. Wyatt had a special kind of calm about him, a confidence, Elsie guessed, that seemed to rub off on her. She felt safer when she was with him, braver.

But was *that* safe? She couldn't afford to get her heart broken and already she could feel fascination with him growing. The image of his eyes, kind and intriguing, flashed into her consciousness.

Exhaling slowly, Elsie did her best to put it all out of her mind. Nothing was going to make sense to her tonight—there was no amount of thinking or overthinking that she could do. Relieved, she felt herself start to drift off.

The voice from her past, the man who'd been in her house, echoed loudly in her mind.

Who was searching for her? Why had they been searching?

And how did that tie into the darkness she remembered as a kid? The closet where she'd been…playing? Hiding?

Yelling.

What had she experienced as a young toddler? And was it going to impact the rest of her life?

Elsie woke when the weight that had been stretched across her legs went away. Willow must have lain down across her, she thought wearily as she struggled to wake up. Then she remembered all the events of the last few days and her eyes shot open.

She glanced at her watch. Just before 5:00 a.m. She'd had maybe four hours of sleep. Not enough, but more than she'd expected to get. She'd take it. Swinging her legs over the side of the bed, she went through the motions of dressing for the day, gathering the gear she'd need. She and Wyatt hadn't discussed what time they'd be leaving, but the day before it had been seven. She wanted to be ready if he showed up early.

At six, Trooper Holland called to let her know they'd canvassed the area and found no evidence of the shooter. They were willing to let the search continue, and that was enough for Elsie. If someone died because of her, which was how this would feel, she might never forgive herself.

That someone out there wanted her dead and may have been involved in the disappearance of the person she was now charged with seeking registered, but only somewhat. She still felt responsible.

Heaviness felt like a cold weight on her this morning. Elsie attempted to settle her mind with yoga, which helped but not enough.

That was how Wyatt found her, standing on her yoga mat in the center of the small cabin, hoping that one more mountain pose would settle her mind.

"I knocked," he said, voice nervous, "but you didn't hear me. I don't know if I should have come in, but the door was unlocked…"

His worries were written on his face, the things unsaid clear to Elsie. He hadn't known what to expect. She felt bad she'd caused him so much anxiety.

"I left it unlocked after I let Willow out this morning," she admitted, realizing even before she offered the explanation that it was a bad one. There was nothing that excused that level of carelessness for her safety.

"Hey, can't change it now," he said in a tone that was once again oddly reassuring to her. "Just do better next time." Wyatt studied her for a minute and Elsie had to fight the urge to shrink away from his scrutiny. What would he notice in her expression, which she didn't seem able to guard to her usual ability?

"I just…" How to even explain? "I don't feel good about all of this."

"Have you prayed about it?"

"No." She didn't hesitate to answer, thinking the question was strange coming from Wyatt, even though he'd grown up in a really religious family. "Do you think that actually works?"

"I'm sure it does."

Speechless was an understatement. Elsie truly didn't know what to say to that.

"You're surprised." Wyatt's voice wasn't judgmental, but he seemed surprised by her reaction. "You're not a believer?"

That was a strange way to phrase it. "Like, in Jesus or Christianity or something?"

"Yeah." His soft laugh wasn't at her, somehow disarming her when she'd been ready to be defensive. "That's okay, Elsie. I'm not, like, weirded out. I just always assumed. Lindsay talks about her faith all the time, and you're best friends." He shrugged. "I assumed and shouldn't have."

"I think people have to decide for themselves what they believe."

"I agree."

She'd expected judgment or an argument and wasn't getting it. It almost frustrated her more than the uncomfortable feeling she'd had all morning.

"I'm praying about this case," Wyatt finally said. "I'm not sure if it helps or hurts to know that, but I wanted you to know."

"I appreciate it, I guess. I don't know. If it makes you feel better..." She trailed off. Might something like that make *her* feel better? But that sounded like using religion as a crutch, and she was too strong for that. Plus, if God was real, if He was the God Lindsay believed Him to be, and apparently Wyatt, too, then it seemed insulting to reduce Him to a "crutch." She and Lindsay had talked about faith enough over the years that Elsie would definitely say she believed in God, probably even the God the Bible described. But while she could respect Him, the idea of having any kind of relationship or interaction with Him seemed weird.

"It does. When do you want to leave this morning? I wasn't sure, so I tried to get here early."

Her mind still spinning, trying to make sense of his reaction, which was not what she'd expected, Elsie struggled to get her bearings. "Yeah, same, I wasn't sure… I made coffee." She cleared her throat, willed herself to get it together. "Would you like a cup?"

"I'd love one," he said with a smile, and Elsie felt herself relax, just a little. The threat against her was still real and her anxiety loomed large and intimidating. But with Wyatt's smile, and maybe with the faith she could kind of sense around him…somehow she felt a little less hopeless than she'd felt when she'd woken up.

She could only hope the moment of relative peace lasted, even though she was fairly certain it couldn't. Nothing like that ever did.

SEVEN

"She's got a scent." Elsie's voice was almost sparkling with excitement. She picked up her pace and Wyatt followed, hurrying into the dark woods, despite his misgivings about Elsie putting herself at risk. It seemed reckless for her to walk back into the woods that had proved so dangerous yesterday, but he understood her reasoning. Still, he wasn't about to let her out of his sight today on a search, and he'd brought his revolver today as an extra precaution.

So far it had been a morning of ups and downs. It almost felt as if they'd shared something like a moment at her cabin, when he'd found her doing yoga and they'd had that brief conversation about faith. Wyatt had been surprised to hear that Elsie didn't share his and Lindsay's faith, but it didn't change his view of her, really. He wished for her sake that she knew God, since he knew how much his own life had been made better by a genuine relationship with Him.

Then they'd flown to the island and met up with the state troopers, who had spent the night on the island in a makeshift command center they'd set up on the beach. The two officers from yesterday had been joined by several more, and one of them had met Elsie at the beach when they'd arrived with a manila envelope and a plastic bag with some kind of cloth in it, presumably something that had belonged to the victim. She'd spent a few minutes looking at the pages and mumbling to herself. Wyatt had figured it was best not to interrupt her, and then they'd taken off into the woods.

"How do you know she's got a scent?" he asked now.

"'Cause she told me."

Well. Obviously. He should have known. Wyatt grinned. "No, I mean—" he exhaled as they ran "—how did she tell you? I didn't see her do anything."

"She barked and took off. That's her alert."

"And she's searching specifically for the missing person today?"

"Right. The troopers were able to get me more search data, including information on who she is and even something with her scent on it to smell."

It seemed like it had paid off somehow because Willow was alert, clearly on the trail, and Elsie all but sparkled as she followed her.

They wound up toward the higher elevations of the island, crossing a small stream and stepping over countless roots. The woods and brush were thinner up here. He wondered if the missing person had tried to find a cell signal or something. That would be a pretty reasonable explanation for the scent going uphill.

Or trying to escape from someone.

They followed Willow for at least half an hour until the dog's pace slowed, and she turned back to Elsie with a look that must have been something, because Elsie suggested they take a break.

"So what did you learn about the missing person?" Wyatt asked when they'd been sitting for a minute. He didn't even have a name to mentally call the person, which seemed strange.

Elsie took a bite of her granola bar, chewed for a minute, seeming lost in thought, which made sense to Wyatt. While he knew the information packet had helped Elsie, it still must be odd to distill a person down into a few notes and bullet points here and there. Maybe she was mentally sorting through what she knew, finding which high points to hit for him.

"Noelle Mason. She's from Anchorage. Pretty young, only twenty-three."

"That is young. What does she do?"

"Works at a homeless resource center in Anchorage, actually."

"Was she hiking alone?"

Elsie frowned. "No, with a friend. But the friend returned—Rebecca Reyes, according to the packet I got—and she left without Noelle, which seems odd. The friend reported her missing." She finished the granola bar.

"You'd think the friend would have stayed on the island, maybe, and waited for Noelle? And how had they been separated in the first place?"

"Assuming they hired a water taxi to drop them off here like a lot of hikers do, it's possible they got separated and Rebecca didn't want to miss the water taxi… Still, it seems odd."

"What are you thinking happened?" Wyatt asked.

She shook her head.

"I don't know… It doesn't make a lot of sense." She

shook her head, but the tension in her face and slight wrinkle in her forehead remained.

Wyatt reached for the trash, handed her a water bottle, which she took with a surprised look. "Thank you." She took a long drink.

"She has no family. She was reported missing by the friend who had been hiking with her the day before…"

"At least no one is looking for her. Family-wise, I mean."

The words were no sooner out of his mouth than Wyatt felt like a cold breeze had separated him and Elsie. She narrowed her eyes at him.

"What do you mean?"

"Just that if she doesn't have a family, it's good there's not a whole family out there worried…" Yeah, he wasn't making this better. It was a hollow reassurance, one of those ridiculous things people said to make other people feel better when something awful had happened. Even if she didn't have a family missing her, it was terrible that she was missing. There were other people in her life whom her loss would impact. Coworkers. Maybe clients at the homeless shelter.

He'd messed up.

"Elsie, listen."

She did not seem eager to listen.

He couldn't blame her.

He hadn't meant the words to sound callous. Of *course* he believed every life had value and that what Elsie was doing was worth it, though it was hard for him to see her risking her life for *anyone*. But he didn't expect her to understand that and, well, he'd messed up. Badly.

Beside him, Willow lay on the ground, seeming to give him a look that conveyed her displeasure with him. Elsie was poring over the manila envelope, apparently not feeling like she'd had enough time to look at the profile before they'd jumped into searching.

He needed to apologize but didn't know how to convince her that he meant it. He'd been good with words once upon a time, but it was like when he'd turned his life around God had taken away a bit of his ability to talk himself out of any trouble. Or into trouble. Which was good, but it definitely made moments like this harder, when he felt like he was fumbling for words.

"Elsie, I need you to hear me. I didn't mean it the way it sounded."

This time, she looked up at him, maybe hearing in his voice the fact that he was genuine. He waited for her to speak, holding his breath, realizing how much her friendship, if that was what you could call it, was starting to mean to him, even after such a short time.

"So you didn't mean it wasn't worth looking for her or anything like that?" Elsie didn't like how doubtful she sounded, but at the same time, she wasn't sure she liked her willingness to hear Wyatt out. The words had obviously been careless, and Wyatt had done nothing to make her think that some people had more value than others. But his words hit close to home.

Was *she* worth finding? After all, no one was looking for her. No one except someone who apparently wanted her dead. Of course Wyatt didn't know that, couldn't, since she'd kept that information from him.

Without thinking, she turned to him. "I told you I was in foster care."

"Yeah."

"Because they never could figure out who I belonged to. Who I was." She swallowed hard. "The OCS case-worker liked the name Elsie. She was from Montgomery. Through a series of what I'm sure were annoying legal hoops, that became my name." Elsie made herself not look away, kept his gaze. Saw his eyes...

Shine with tears?

"Elsie, I had no idea. I'm sorry that happened to you." He blinked, and the shine was gone. Maybe she'd been imagining it. But his voice sounded sincere. "I had no idea. Wow, no wonder you want people found."

She hated how easily he understood her.

Yes, she was still waiting to be found herself. Not by this would-be killer. But by someone. Had someone cared about her, ever? The holes in her past weren't an absence; they were a presence all their own, haunting her life.

"Anyway." Elsie cleared her throat, stacking up the papers she'd been looking at. "I'm almost ready to keep going. I think if Willow could find the scent again, we might make more progress today."

"Why did she lose it, do you know?"

"Could be any number of things." Elsie looked around. "The trees are a little thinner this high up, the vegetation, too. That makes the scent less likely to be trapped." She frowned. "That's my best guess. A shift in the wind? Scent is a fascinating thing."

"I'm amazed you can do all this."

She raised her eyebrows.

"Not that I'm surprised you specifically can do this, just that it's a thing at all. It's like you can read the dog's mind and she can read the wind, the air itself. That's pretty amazing, that's all. Your dog's amazing. You're…" Wyatt trailed off.

The silence stretched between them and Elsie heard every noise. The wind in the spruce trees below them, the sound of Willow's breathing, her own heartbeat pounding in her ears.

The thing that scared her most was that Wyatt didn't sound like he was feeding her lines. He sounded awfully sincere. Surely she was intelligent enough that she could tell if someone was genuine.

But she didn't trust herself right now, not with her old high school crush coming back to life. Even when he'd not been her type, when he'd been living life at way too fast a pace, she'd been intrigued by Wyatt. It had been so easy as a teenager to write that off to a stereotypical attraction to the bad boy, heightened by the fact that he was her friend's very much off-limits brother.

But she wasn't a high school kid anymore, and Wyatt wasn't the man he'd been. And she liked who he seemed to be now. Not just a high school bad-boy stereotype, but a man who wanted to keep her safe even if it meant stepping into danger. A man who liked her dog. Someone who would follow instructions on a search without trying to pretend like he was the one in charge.

She…liked him. A lot. More than she had meant to?

That was almost as scary as anything that could be waiting for them in this wilderness. Even Elsie's past.

"We should go. Start the search again," she said quietly, but the words still felt so loud to her own ears as she broke the silence and whatever might have been between them.

Wyatt started to stand as soon as she said the words. "Sounds good."

If only Elsie felt like anything was normal between them. She put Willow's vest back on, told her to continue the search and then followed, aware of Wyatt's presence close behind or even beside her. He was quiet. More so than he'd been on the way this morning, but maybe he was getting tired.

Or maybe she wasn't the only one aware of…whatever it was. The fact that he'd almost called her amazing, then cut himself off. It wasn't like he'd confessed his undying love. He hadn't even tried to kiss her, like those moments characters in a movie had where they moved close and their lips parted and all of that ridiculousness.

Somehow it was more than that, though. The catch in his voice, the genuine admiration, even if he hadn't finished his thought… It meant more to Elsie than all those things.

She hurried through the woods, eyes on Willow, willing herself to see something that could help them in their search for the missing woman. Noelle Mason, twenty-three. Orphan, no family. Worked in Anchorage at a community homelessness resource center, volunteered at elections, snowboarder, hiker.

The details made her more vivid in Elsie's mind, less ethereal. This was a real human they were searching for, which was why it was so important not to let the search slack off at all, even if one's search partner had dark eyes and a too-appealing five-o'clock shadow.

Willow sniffed at the air at their next decision point,

where the trail split in two directions. Elsie waited as Willow considered her options, then seemed to catch just a hint of scent with her nose and took off toward the right.

"Is this a fast search or a slow one?" Wyatt asked as they kept following her.

"Most searches are over pretty quickly, statistically speaking. But here in Alaska it seems like we often get the searches that last for multiple days."

"Just the terrain difference, you think?"

"That and maybe we have different categories of people getting lost? It's really difficult to say." She shook her head. "I don't know, really."

"Do you think…?" His voice trailed off. "I mean, she could still be alive."

"Yes, definitely. It's a good time of year to survive in some ways, dangerous in others. If she's gotten rain-soaked or wet somehow, then hypothermia is a legitimate worry, even though it's not necessarily cold outside. But if she's managed to stay dry, this is definitely not too long."

"And we don't know if the shooter is still here. Do you think…? Is she connected to that?"

Elsie hadn't managed to work that out.

How *was* the missing person connected to the people who appeared to be after Elsie? She had to admit that this seemed too big a coincidence for there not to be a connection.

"I don't know. What do you think?"

"I wouldn't know where to start coming up with ideas about something like that…" He trailed off. "It really might be time to talk to the police."

"No."

"The troopers, then."

"Still no."

"Elsie…"

"I told you, Wyatt, they'll take me off the case and there's no one else around here. She needs to be found."

"She's not the only one. You need to be able to find out what's going on and move on without this shadow hanging over you and some kind of mysterious past hunting you down."

"Hey, leave my past out of it." Her voice was firm. Resolute. "This is *my* life and I don't want them digging deeper into it."

"Because you're afraid of what they'll find?"

"Absolutely yes." She met his stare, looked back firmly, then directed her attention to the dog. "I don't need someone else digging into a past I don't know enough about myself."

She read his hesitation and doubt in her plan, but so far he wasn't convinced enough that she was wrong to go against her wishes, which she appreciated.

"How about we go over it tonight? When we're back in town, when it's too late to search for the day, let's see if we can come up with some ideas."

"That'll mean me digging into your past, won't it?"

That was different. Or was it? She could trust Wyatt, Elsie knew that.

She took a breath. "I think that's a risk I'm willing to take."

Hopefully it was a smart one, one that would lead to removing the threat against her and not one that would result in getting her heart broken.

With every step, she felt her sense of unease grow,

but she didn't think it had to do with Wyatt. Elsie mentally ran through lists of possibilities, finally realizing it was something about the way Willow was holding herself. She was still searching, very much at work, but something in the tilt of her ears said she was listening, too, and not just for any commands Elsie might give her.

What did she hear? Not their missing person, or she'd have alerted by now. A dog's hearing was incredible, and so was their sense of smell.

"I don't think we're alone," she whispered to Wyatt, wanting him to be prepared. She stopped, and he hesitated alongside her, close enough she could have reached out and touched him. She could feel him tensing, could feel it in herself as well.

EIGHT

Wyatt didn't know how long they'd stood there, but after a short bit of time—two minutes? Ten?—Elsie blew out a breath and shook her head. "It's gone now. I have no idea what she was hearing."

More like *who*. Despite the troopers' belief that the shooter had taken off, chances were high that they weren't alone on the island, not even with the missing woman. Someone *else* was here, on the island with them.

They searched for hours, Wyatt doing his best to help Elsie where he could. He watched her, captivated by her work and the way she interacted with her dog, and finally started to feel like he was able to support her and not just follow along behind her.

For example, he'd started to notice the way her jaw would tighten. Sometimes because Willow had picked up a scent, or maybe lost it, and sometimes because she was hungry. He'd learned that if Willow needed something, food or water, Elsie was quick to stop, but she didn't always take the time to take care of herself. Wyatt made it his mission to help her take care of herself as well, or at least let him take care of her.

She seemed to have forgiven him for his careless words earlier, for which he was thankful. He was still struggling to wrap his mind around what she'd told him about her own life and background. So Elsie had no family. At least, none that she knew of. That painted everything in a different light. Every time she'd come to his and Lindsay's parents' house for Thanksgiving after she'd turned eighteen...or worse, every time that she *hadn't*... So then where had she gone, whom had she been with?

He thought of the way her cabin was so isolated, like that was what she expected out of life. She'd probably been alone.

As a teenager, he'd been annoyed by her. Wasn't that practically a rule, to find your sister's best friend annoying? He'd resented her presence at holiday functions because, after all, she wasn't *family*.

Now he wasn't sure he had even known what that word had meant back then. Because of course she was family. Lindsay was the closest thing to family that she had.

Wyatt noticed Elsie pulling ahead of him again and he picked up the pace, dodging around a spruce tree and narrowly avoiding being smacked in the face by one of its dark green branches. She was able to dodge in and out of trees as gracefully as if she'd been raised in the woods, and in some ways maybe she had.

He wasn't being honest with himself, Wyatt knew. Sure, he'd been annoyed by her presence when he was younger, but wasn't some of that because in addition to his stereotypical dislike of his sister's friend...he'd also had a bit of a stereotypical attraction to her? She'd not been his type at all, but something about her drew him. Even then, he knew she was too good for him and it made him aggravated.

Adult Elsie was *definitely* too good for him, but adult Wyatt wished she weren't, because he was thinking if he'd ever had a different type before, he'd been entirely wrong. How could anything be more attractive than a woman like Elsie—let's be honest, *Elsie*, not just a woman like her—able to hike through the woods with more grace than a wild animal, brown hair tangling in curls behind her, petite and delicate but not afraid of anything, at least not that Wyatt could tell.

She was brave and smart and beautiful.

The shadows were lengthening by the time Elsie started to slow down. He hadn't suggested they stop for hours, but was about to when she turned around and shook her head. "She lost the scent."

"When?"

"Just now. Did you notice we slowed down a quarter mile back or so? I was trying to help Willow pick it up again."

"Should we go back to there?"

Elsie seemed to be considering. "Could I see a map?"

He handed it to her. She traced a finger along their route. They'd gone up the mountain earlier, then down and into this hollow where they now found themselves, surrounded by trees and vegetation. It was the perfect place for someone to hide. Or be hidden by someone else. Dense and wild. It made Wyatt uneasy. He much preferred the beach area where the plane was, or even the higher mountain areas. He was a pilot. He naturally wanted to have a view, so he couldn't imagine someone hiding down here on purpose.

"If we go back toward where we lost her scent..." Her voice trailed off. "Maybe? I think it's worth it. Then from there we'd better head back to the plane."

"I agree." There was plenty of light, but Wyatt knew they had a while to hike before they made it back to the plane.

They started walking and Elsie stopped him and pointed when they reached the fork in the trail where they'd lost the scent.

"I think maybe she didn't take a trail from here? But walked through the trees instead."

"Why?"

"Just a guess."

They stood for a minute, Wyatt lost in his own thoughts, not able to guess at what Elsie might be thinking. Then the hair on his arms stood up.

He looked over at Elsie to see if she'd noticed... whatever it was. She'd stilled also, as had Willow.

"What is it?" He chanced a whisper, not sure for his part if they were dealing with human threat or animal. Grizzly bears did stalk this part of the Alaskan wilderness, their paws bigger than a man's face and unspeakably damaging. It could easily be a bear they'd sensed, even if Wyatt wasn't sure exactly what it was he'd noticed. A smell? A noise?

It was more of a presence. An awareness that they weren't alone.

Elsie moved forward, toward Willow, who had turned back toward Wyatt.

"Wyatt, no!"

Her scream registered at the same moment he felt something hard slam into his head. Blinded by the pain, he threw his arms out, tried to fight back, but darkness was already closing in. No, no, no, he could not afford to lose consciousness right now.

"Elsie, run!" he managed to yell before he went to his knees, the explosion of pain coming in echoes across his entire head. He laid his head on the ground, struggling to maintain consciousness, and after a second or two managed to stand back up. In the brief struggle, and his own pain, he'd lost sight of Elsie, his assailant, Willow, everyone.

God, help me find her again, he prayed and started down the trail. As he ran, he winced against the throbs of pain in his head and blinked away something that was obscuring his vision. He held a hand to his forehead, then drew it away. Shiny blood streaked across his hand.

He was mad enough to spit. How had he missed that someone was lurking close enough by to attack him?

And why hit him rather than just shoot him? He was thankful, but didn't know why the method of attack concerned him.

Where. Was. Elsie?

That was what concerned him most, the confirmation that whoever was after her was still very much on her tail and somewhere on the island. Right now, very close to her. Pursuing her.

Unless he'd already caught her.

Wyatt wished he had Willow with him, though he knew he wouldn't be able to read her cues and he certainly didn't wish Elsie was without her. But they'd gotten separated at a split in the trail and he had no idea which way Elsie would have gone. He stopped. Stared. Thought, *tried* to think like Elsie would have.

Back to the plane. He felt confident in his decision. It was where she'd run yesterday, and it made sense. He kept going, changing directions slightly to head back toward the beach, praying that he was right.

He was nearing a thick stand of spruce trees when he felt like he was being watched. Still irritated he'd been taken off guard earlier, he pulled his revolver out of its holster. He was not going to be attacked again, and he was *going* to find Elsie.

Holding his breath, he stepped into the darkness of the forest.

"Wyatt." The voice was a whisper. Elsie's. Her arm reached out of the trees and pulled him in.

Her eyes were wide and she was holding Willow close to her, but they both appeared uninjured.

"You're bleeding," she told him, her voice quiet, wavering.

"I'm fine. I'm more focused on the fact that you're okay." Wyatt felt like he could breathe again.

"We ran, like you said. Willow held him off while I ran and then she caught up to me. I can't believe I left her. I shouldn't have left her…"

"Did you tell her to come?"

"Yes."

"Elsie, that's the most obedient dog I've ever known. If she wouldn't listen to you, she was *sure* about it. You can't force her not to try to protect you."

Willow seemed to agree with him, her eyes meeting his. Wyatt would have sworn at the moment the dog could talk and was thanking him for taking her side.

"I'm just glad she's okay." Her arms tightened around the dog. "But your head…"

"You're a first responder. You know head wounds bleed a lot."

"You can't fly us out of here."

"If we need to get out, I'll get us out." His voice was probably gruffer than he'd meant for it to be.

She didn't try to argue with him there, which he appreciated, but the truth was his head was throbbing from the hit and his mind felt like cotton balls had been stashed in it. Thinking felt oddly harder than it should, like his mental engine took a moment of revving before firing up. He'd had a concussion before—baseball in high school—and it had felt just like this. He didn't know how he was going to safely fly them both back. Realistically, he couldn't. He'd have to figure something else out. Surely he knew someone else with a seaplane. Or the troopers could call someone.

This complicated their search, for sure. No one would call him fit to fly at the moment, or even in the coming week, or even longer. Most of the concussion protocols he'd heard of involved a month out of a plane.

Nothing he could do to change it.

"Do you know where he went?" he asked, directing the conversation back to whoever was on the island with them.

"I don't." Her voice trembled. "I just dove in here to hide."

Wyatt hated that she sounded scared. He wanted to do everything in his power to keep her from being afraid.

But with someone in the woods who clearly wanted them stopped, he understood her fear. It was probably very much justified.

* * *

He'd said he was fine, but Elsie wasn't sure she really believed him, which was why she'd insisted that Wyatt ·walk ahead of her. Enough time had passed since the initial injury that she didn't think he'd pass out, but you just never knew with head trauma.

Speaking of trauma, she'd noticed her hands were shaking. Adrenaline, most likely. But knowing the reason for it didn't make it any less scary. She didn't like admitting that what she'd experienced affected her at all, and she had lived in denial for years about her childhood affecting her, but there would be no denying that this was going to.

The fact that he hadn't argued much about walking in front of her was scaring Elsie. As protective as he'd been about her safety, almost to the point of treating her too carefully, she'd expected him to put up a fight and demand to be in the back in case danger came from that direction. Maybe he was telling himself that being in front of her was keeping her safe, too. At the moment, Elsie didn't care too much about her safety. She was worried about Wyatt.

Entirely more worried than she'd have thought she would be. Not just because he was supposed to have been her ride home, but because she cared about him, and at the sight of him being attacked by someone—she'd seen no identifying features since the person had been wearing a ski mask—she'd realized just how much she cared about him.

"You still okay up there?" she asked, deliberately keeping her voice calm as they made their way back down the trail toward the airplane.

"Yeah. Fine."

Less talkative than earlier. She noted that out of purely medical concern.

Although she could hardly justify her desire to reach out and comfort him, maybe stroke her hand across the uninjured half of his forehead, tell him it was going to be okay. None of that was particularly professional.

Wyatt made the last turn through the woods that would lead them straight back to the beach, and she didn't even bother trying to make any more conversation. With everything that had happened in the last few hours, they were both beyond conversation at this point anyway.

It wasn't until Willow started to sniff that Elsie herself noticed the smell. Smoke. Something was burning.

Stomach churning, worst-case scenarios coming to mind, Elsie stepped in front of Wyatt. "I've got to go see what's going on. Willow smells something."

He was frowning, brows pushed together, and he nodded. "Me, too."

Elsie picked up her pace and followed her dog, this time making careful note that Wyatt was right behind them as well. So far he seemed okay, steady enough to walk on his own.

"I'm fine, Elsie. Go. I can keep up."

The man clearly wasn't used to being a liability and it rubbed him wrong. Interesting. The Wyatt she'd known before wouldn't have been this determined to help, or understanding enough to not slow her down. He'd been so much more concerned with his own interests and pursuits, but it was just one more confirmation that the Wyatt she'd known before was gone, replaced by this newer, better version.

One far more dangerous for her heart.

Something inside her had *always* warned of danger in getting close to anyone like that. Being someone's friend was one thing, though she'd readily admit she held herself back in friendships, too. But being someone's romantic partner?

Terror. Because of her past? The dark? The yelling? Or because she was just afraid?

Elsie hated to be afraid.

She pushed ahead, running toward the scent of the smoke, grateful to notice somewhat morbidly that it didn't smell like burning human remains. Despite Willow's eagerness to reach the source of the smell, and the fact that she *did* have training as an HR, Human Remains, dog as well as search and rescue, Elsie didn't think her attitude was quite right for that. Something else was burning. On the beach, beyond the thickness and darkness of the woods.

A step into the clearing revealed what it was.

Wyatt's airplane.

The front of it, where they'd sat just hours before, was engulfed in flames. Elsie stopped walking. Stunned.

Bumping into her arm slightly as he stumbled past, Wyatt hurried toward the plane.

"No, don't!" she yelled, but stopped herself from saying more. Somehow, she understood. The plane wasn't alive like her dog was, but it was his partner in a similar way. It was part of what he did every day. More than that, part of who he was.

Thankfully, rather than run directly at the flames, he'd gone to the back of the plane, which wasn't yet burning.

He emerged from the smoke with a bucket, ran to the shore and started throwing water onto the plane. Elsie moved in his direction.

"Stay back!"

She stopped where she was, a hand on Willow's vest, and hoped this wasn't a losing battle. After several trips, she thought she saw the flames beaten back slightly. Willow cried on occasion, a sad, low pitch.

Elsie wanted to cry, too.

Wyatt kept going until the fire was out. The back three-fourths of the plane were mostly fine, but the fire had fully engulfed the seats, the controls, those things that would be desperately needed to fly them home.

"I'm going to call someone to get us out of here," Wyatt said after a moment, his voice rough from the smoke.

"Your plane..." She trailed off, unable to formulate her thoughts. What did one say to this loss?

His jaw was tight, his eyes flashing with anger. "My plane is just an object. But someone is determined to harm you. First they attack us, then burn the plane? I have to get you out of here." He raked a hand through his hair, pacing the beach. "The troopers. Call the troopers, tell them to send someone as soon as possible."

Needing something to do, feeling too outside of her comfort zone, Elsie nodded and pulled out her phone, reported the details as best she could and winced at the reply.

"It could be a while," she turned to Wyatt and said softly after she'd hung up. "Most of their resources around here are focused on a rescue taking place closer to home. The troopers who were here earlier got called away to deal with that."

"Not acceptable." His jaw clenched and unclenched, and Elsie reached for his arm, laid her hand on it.

Like it was slow motion, like a scene in a movie where the music started to drive faster and louder, Wyatt looked down at her hand. It took all the bravery she possessed not to move it, not to move at all. He reached up his other hand, laid it on top of hers.

"I'm not going to let anything happen to you."

Her own frustration rose within her. "It's not just me here, okay? You're here, too, and you've lost too much already because of me. You're hurt. Now your plane..." Her words were choked and she swallowed back her tears, afraid if she let them fall she'd be powerless to stop them. Worse than this show of vulnerability was the fact that Wyatt didn't seem fazed by it. It affected him, she could tell that by the way his hold on her had tightened, squeezed, but he wasn't scared.

That scared her almost as much as whoever was after her.

NINE

Night crept up on you this time of year, when summer was over but winter hadn't yet tightened its grip on the land. Wyatt and Elsie sat, backs to the plane, looking out over the choppy gray waters of the Gulf of Alaska. He was pretty sure Elsie had been crying earlier, and equally sure that she'd been crying for *him*.

How could she think he was the one to feel sorry for? He tightened his arm a little bit. Pulled her a little closer. They'd started sitting like this maybe half an hour ago, huddled together for warmth, his arm around her shoulders.

He'd warmed up long ago and she wasn't shivering anymore, either, but still, Wyatt hadn't let go. And Elsie hadn't moved away.

"Surely someone will be here soon," he said even as he considered the darkening gray of the sky. If the Troopers weren't sending someone out tonight, there was a chance no local pilots would be willing to fly with these clouds moving in. Many people in Alaska had private pilot licenses but weren't instrument rated, which they had to be to be able to fly by sight.

Wyatt may have said encouraging words, but the longer they sat on the damp, rocky beach, the more convinced he became that they may not be leaving that night.

"You really think so?" Elsie shifted toward him, and she was so close he could smell her shampoo. It was something citrusy, orange or grapefruit, and it smelled like sunshine.

He couldn't lie to her.

So he didn't try. "No, I don't. I was trying to be positive."

"Yeah, I don't think so, either." She sighed, then sat in silence for a second before scooting away from his arm and angling herself to face him. "I vote we camp here by the plane. It's better visibility both for when someone does come for us, hopefully tomorrow, and it gives us sort of a barrier zone where we can see if someone is coming." She looked out toward the trees. "Usually I would like the safety of the woods, but I think being out in the open is safer tonight."

"I agree. I had a tent, but it didn't survive the fire." He'd made a quick inventory of his storage area when it was safe to do so. Some items were fine, but the tent was not.

"I have tarps and some emergency bivy sacks in my backpack."

Of course she did. Elsie was the kind of SAR worker who would be prepared for anything, and that included possibly having to stay overnight in the wilderness. The tarps they could use to make a tent, and the bivy sacks, like ultrathin, disposable sleeping bags, would keep them warm and insulate them against the elements.

"Sounds like a plan."

She moved to her backpack and started pulling things out, and Wyatt kept an eye on the woods, not willing to let his guard down even for a few minutes. Willow, he'd noticed, was lying near Elsie's backpack, watching the woods as well. Wyatt's head still throbbed, a reminder of how easily someone could sneak up on them.

Less so here, but in exchange, they'd make easy targets for a gunman. Was it possible the shooter had lost his gun, and that was why he'd hit Wyatt instead?

"I'm sorry about your plane," she said as they worked.

"It's okay." Wyatt was surprised at how true the words felt. "It was insured. It'll work out. Better the plane than you." Compared with the thought that someone could have harmed Elsie, the plane just didn't mean as much.

"What made you want to become a pilot, anyway?" she asked, looking over at him.

His shoulders tensed. Everything related to his past made him tense, and he took a breath to relax his muscles. Elsie had shared enough about herself; surely he could return the favor.

"Well, I sort of decided college wasn't for me. I liked what I was learning…" he started.

"What was that?"

"Psychology." He watched her for any kind of reaction, surprise that a guy like him who hadn't taken school too seriously would ever think he could study something like psychology. The truth was that while he'd squeaked by with several Ds in core classes in school, he'd gotten an A in psychology because he liked it. People intrigued him.

"Sounds interesting," she said.

"It was… But I was spending too much time partying. Not enough studying. I flunked out."

There was no surprise on her face now, but neither was there the judgment he'd been expecting. Instead she was just watching him, waiting for him to tell her the rest of it.

"I came back up here, started doing odd jobs for a friend of the family, cleaning his plane, his hangar… Eventually I decided I'd better do something with my life. I got my private pilot's license, moved up from there in hours and certifications, and here we are." He shrugged. "Could you hand me that tarp?" he asked, abruptly changing the subject.

Within half an hour, they had their shelter set up, and night had finished falling, dark clouds stealing the light even earlier than usual. The lack of daylight was disconcerting, even though it was well past 9:00 p.m. Wyatt and Elsie both climbed under the tarp they'd set up. It would protect them from any rain, but the sides were open.

"Kinda tight inside our little temporary home here," Wyatt joked, poking at the low roof of the tarp.

"Definitely not five-star accommodations. I mean, look at this view. Just monotonous. Wave after wave," she teased back, motioning to their spectacular ocean view. They'd set up a bit away from the plane, to make sure they were well past the high-tide mark. Neither of them wanted to wake up to ocean waves lapping at their feet.

He laughed at her words. "Surely you've slept in worse places, doing the job you do."

"Oh, definitely." She hesitated. "Never with anyone after me, though."

"So this is new?"

"Yeah. New experience for sure." Her eyes flicked to his, and Wyatt could have almost sworn he saw more in them.

He was no stranger to seeing a spark of interest in a woman's eyes, but it had been so long. Years since he'd dated at all, since his self-imposed exile from the dating scene while he tried to get his life together. And then years of feeling like he had something to prove, like it wasn't worth the risk of turning back into who he used to be. Was he just out of practice that he thought he saw that same spark in Elsie's eyes?

No, he didn't think so. Would he be out of line to tell her he cared more about her than he was trying to let on? No, he still couldn't. She was in danger and needed to focus on that. Besides, could he really risk making things awkward when they were trapped out here alone together?

She looked away, then said, "Who takes the first watch?"

He cleared his throat, trying to ignore the way his heart was pounding. "I think I should stay awake for the night and you should try to sleep, so you're ready to search again whenever you can."

"That's a no. You've already gotten involved in a fight that wasn't yours and spent all day helping me search in rough terrain. I'm not going to just lie down and sleep while you keep us safe, too. You can't do it *all*, Wyatt."

See, he'd have said it was Elsie doing more than her fair share.

"Okay, we'll take turns," he said, agreeing to her suggestion.

"You sleep first," she said, as he'd expected, but Wyatt was ready.

"I have a concussion, so I should stay awake for now." He grinned at her. "You'd better go first."

He'd never seen someone roll her eyes so cutely before.

"You're a pilot. You must have enough first aid training to know that medical experts no longer recommend keeping a concussion patient awake."

"Better safe than sorry?"

Elsie yawned, tried to catch herself.

"Seriously. Sleep, Elsie. You've worked hard."

From where she lay curled up, Willow seemed to agree that Elsie needed to sleep. Her dark eyes were wide and fixed on Elsie.

Elsie noticed, too, because she called her dog to her. Willow obeyed and she rubbed the dog's thick white fur. "A nap. I will take a nap. Two hours, max."

"Fine. Two hours."

She was asleep within minutes, leaving Wyatt alone to think about who could be after her and why. And what he could do to help. How would they investigate who she'd been decades ago when she had no ties to her old life, no inkling of where she'd come from?

How did she handle not having any links to her past? He wondered if she'd experienced trauma at a young age. Considering the danger she was in now, maybe it was better that she *didn't* have those links.

The time went by quickly in the quiet of night, as Wyatt kept his eyes open and his ears tuned to any unusual sounds in the woods. After two hours had passed, he debated not waking Elsie, but knew she'd be frustrated if he didn't stick to the plan. So he reached for her shoulder and gently nudged it.

She was awake in seconds, eyes wide, blinking.

"It's your turn. But if you'd rather keep sleeping…" He let his voice trail off.

She moved into a sitting position, shook her head. "No, I'm good. You take a rest now."

So he lay down on a jacket he'd wadded up to use as a pillow. He knew sleep wouldn't come easily. The pain in his head was less than it had been earlier, but he still wasn't comfortable, and he had too many thoughts running through his mind.

It was enough to overwhelm him if he let it, so Wyatt tried not to focus on it. Tried to just fall asleep. And eventually felt himself drifting off.

Screams tore the air. Panicked screams of pain or terror or possibly both.

Elsie's eyes flew open. She'd thought she'd been awake, but she found herself slumped over and startled by the sound. She'd accidentally fallen asleep during her hour to watch. A couple of feet away from her, Wyatt stirred.

"What's going on?" he whispered.

"I don't know." Humiliated, she admitted, "I fell asleep. I'm sorry."

"Don't be, can't change it now. Was that a woman? Not a bird, some kind of wildlife…?"

Another scream. Indisputably human.

Willow growled.

"What if it's our missing person?" Elsie asked. "Shouldn't we try to save her?"

"You're search and rescue and I'm a pilot. We're not a tactical team. That's a job for SWAT, maybe the Troopers. Us getting hurt or worse won't help her or law enforcement."

She raised her eyebrows.

"Elsie…"

She heard him, she really did. And she seriously considered staying where she was, not risking her life any more than she already had. She had to admit that the person who was after her was here on the island and wanted her dead.

But what if their missing hiker had met with foul play *because* Elsie had been the one sent to search for her? What if her would-be attacker had come upon the missing woman in the woods just now and harmed her, thinking she was Elsie?

It would be difficult if not nearly impossible to live with that on her conscience.

"Elsie… Where are you?"

That voice. It came from the woods. Familiar, threatening, the same she'd heard twice before.

She moved closer to Wyatt. Fear gripped her throat and chest. "That's him."

He pulled a revolver of some sort out of a holster and she felt a small amount of relief. The most dangerous weapon she had on her was bear spray, which would be effective on a human, though technically that use was illegal.

But he didn't shoot it.

"What are you doing?"

"I can't shoot without a target." Frustration colored his tone.

"Where are you, Elsie?" the voice called. "You can't get away this time. He was always going to find you."

She frowned. *He?* The man who was after her was separate from the person who wanted her dead or hurt, it seemed.

Her throat closed a little more and she felt herself struggle to stay calm. To breathe.

"What do we do?" she asked Wyatt, wanting to feel less alone. "Stay here? Run?"

This had seemed like a safe place to spend the night, but now she realized that they were sitting ducks.

But the woods weren't far.

The woman who'd screamed was still out there somewhere, too.

Those facts made Elsie's decision for her. She started to tense. "We have to run," she whispered to Wyatt, knowing Willow would read her movements and respond accordingly.

"Elsie, no—" Wyatt started, but she was already sprinting across the beach for the trees opposite where she thought the attacker was. Willow moved with her, the two of them running for the trees and safety. When she was in the shadows and the darkness, not silhouetted in the moonlight, Elsie started to breathe again. Even more so when she heard Wyatt behind her.

"You should've stayed put."

"The voice was getting closer. He was coming for us." Elsie's sense of powerlessness and frustration overwhelmed her. She knew she'd taken a chance running into the woods for cover, but she wasn't sure it was a bad move. "And we have to find the woman who screamed."

"It could be a trap, you know," Wyatt pointed out, and Elsie knew he could be right. But she didn't think he was.

She gave Willow the command to search, heart still pounding. "Can you make sure no one is following us?" she asked Wyatt. "I need to focus on Willow if we're going to have a chance of finding whoever that was before it's too late for them."

Without any more argument, she made her way through the woods, moving so quietly Elsie was convinced she and Willow weren't making any sound at all. Wyatt wasn't doing a half-bad job, either, especially for someone who wasn't used to this. She pushed a spruce branch out of her way.

Willow stopped. She gave a low moan.

Elsie's breath caught in her throat. It was her alert for human remains. Her shoulders fell. After all of this, after days of doing her best, it wasn't good enough. They'd still failed, and failure here on this island, in this corner of Alaska where her past and present swirled together in an uncomfortable haze, was somehow worse than failure elsewhere.

"She's dead," she said to Wyatt, then followed her dog, needing to finish the job, no matter how much she might wish she didn't have to.

Up ahead, Willow stopped, sat next to what looked in the darkness like a shape on the ground. Elsie fought the urge to vomit as her stomach clenched. This was far from the first body she'd seen, and it likely would not be the last, but she never got used to it.

"Elsie, wait." Wyatt's voice was quiet but firm enough that Elsie stopped without thinking.

He held out a hand, pointed.

She could see it now, too, the wound on the victim's back. Blood matting the moss and clumping in the dirt of the small clearing in the woods where the woman's body lay. A metallic scent hung heavy in the air.

She needed to check for vitals but was bracing herself for the worst.

While she took a breath or two to steady herself, Wyatt stepped forward. "I'll do it." He reached for the woman's arm to feel for a pulse and shook his head.

"She's definitely gone. No pulse at all."

But recently dead, Elsie could see that. She swallowed hard against the sense of hopelessness creeping toward her like the fog had crept onto the beach earlier in the night.

How had it only been hours since they'd sat on the beach together, Wyatt's arm around her? Since she'd felt…safe? Sure, the plane had been half-destroyed and they'd been trapped on an island with someone who they knew for sure was willing to kill, but in those moments, she'd felt peaceful. Maybe she'd even let herself dream about more times like that with Wyatt. But just like she'd known it wouldn't, the peace didn't last. It never did.

"I failed her. I should have found her. If I'd led Willow this way before we started searching, if I'd just searched from a different starting point today…" The excuses wouldn't help, the explanations wouldn't help, but Elsie felt chewed up inside, broken in bits and at a loss as to how to fix it.

"You did your best."

But her best hadn't been good enough.

The darkness of the woods pressed in on her, and instead of it being the comfort she was used to it being, it felt suffocating. Like the darkness of her nightmare, flashback, whatever it was. Elsie stood among the trees but could clearly picture that closet. She was sitting on a pair of shoes and they were digging into her leg. Someone had told her to stay in the closet, she remembered now. She had to be very quiet and stay in the closet. Like a game.

But the crying outside the door wasn't a game. The darkness didn't feel like a game. And when she heard someone scream, Elsie *knew* it wasn't a game and she scooted deeper into the closet and tried to be as still as she could. Once it had gone quiet, she pushed the closet door open, needing to see if the person who'd screamed was okay. A family member? A friend? She didn't know, but adult Elsie was afraid of what child Elsie had found. In the cold night air, Elsie blinked, willed the image to go away.

"Elsie?" Wyatt asked softly.

The smell, the screams. All of it was too familiar, and not just from search and rescue work.

She shook her head. "I don't know." She shook her head again, the images long gone but the discomfort remaining, churning in her stomach from more than the gruesome scene in front of her. "We need to call the Troopers. Let them know." She pulled out her phone and did so.

"Whatever you do," the trooper on the phone said, "be careful. The island might not be safe for you guys.

We'll get someone there as soon as possible. Can you stay near the scene to keep it as secure as possible for us? At least until we are close to arriving?"

It was the last thing Elsie wanted to do, but she understood the reason for it and answered that they would. The trooper asked for coordinates to where they were and Elsie gave them as best she could, based on the map.

They retreated from the body twenty or thirty feet, into the shadow of a massive clump of spruce trees, and Elsie finally felt like she could breathe again. Willow was still beside her, her demeanor subdued, like it was every time she found or was near someone who was deceased.

"Hey, it's okay." Wyatt reached for her hand. In other circumstances, it might have been a romantic moment, but now, as he squeezed her hand, she felt his friendship through the contact.

"It's just all of this. I failed. She's dead, and…" Elsie trailed off.

Did she tell him the rest? Could she trust him? And how did she let him know about this part of herself when she didn't even know what it meant?

She could feel him waiting in the silence. She was waiting, too, to see what happened, to see if she wanted to take another step closer to him or handle this part of her fear alone.

Like she'd always done.

TEN

"I was…" Elsie's words came in starts, her tone shaky. "When we walked up here, something about the smell—the blood, I think—triggered a memory, I guess. Sort of this flashback I've been having. You know in movies where someone hits their head and gets amnesia and then remembers pieces of who they are?"

Wyatt nodded. His sister and mom always had those made-for-TV Christmas movies playing during the holidays. His mom loved a good amnesia story, or war letters, or something that made people cry. "Yeah, I've seen them. Super-feel-good, right? And when the puzzle comes together, there's that whole moment of triumph?"

"Yeah, this is nothing like that." Her voice was sharp-edged. Not bitter necessarily, but hard. "Every time more of this memory comes back, it's worse, it's darker. I don't know what happened before I was left on that island, but it wasn't good."

"Something criminal?"

"I think so. I'm…" She hesitated, and Wyatt didn't know how to encourage her, or if he even should. Neither of them would be able to go back from what she shared. Was he ready to be this much in her past?

She was watching him, like she was waiting for some kind of sign, so he took a deep breath and nodded. "Keep going."

Her words came in a rush then, like a cold wind across him, leaving him chilled. He could only imagine how talking about this, thinking about this, was making Elsie feel.

"I'm in a closet and it's dark. That's all there was for the longest time, this impression of darkness. Then there were voices. Shouting, crying. Just now, tonight…" She trailed off again. "Tonight, there was a scream. Triggered by hearing the woman's screams? I don't know. Maybe that never really happened. Maybe it's not a memory and it's just a weird way of dealing with tonight's trauma, but the smell of blood, the metallic smell, it was familiar. I think… What if I saw someone die?"

"When you were a kid?"

She nodded. "What if that's why someone left me out here? What if I saw something, and even though a three-year-old isn't a reliable witness, maybe it was still too much of a danger for someone?"

It made sense, though it was hard for him to contemplate someone truly being that evil.

But when Wyatt thought of the voice that had been haunting Elsie, the threat of someone finding her, someone who had always been looking for her…

It fit distressingly well.

"Whoa" was all he could say, ineloquent though it was.

"I know." Elsie took a deep breath. "What do I do with that? If this is our missing hiker, then I'm no longer needed here. Which means there's no longer any reason not to tell the Troopers my suspicions. I don't want them looking into my past, but if it brings her killer to justice..." She shook her head. Her head whipped toward his so fast he was surprised she didn't actually give herself whiplash. "Is it my fault she's dead?"

"Surely not. No. Even if it has anything to do with you, the killer made the choice, not you, Elsie."

She seemed to be considering, sitting there quietly with Willow beside her.

"Wyatt?"

"Yeah?"

"Can I ask you something?"

"Sure. Anything," he said, meaning it.

After what she'd just shared, after the way she'd finally fully accepted his help despite how hard it had seemed for her, he wanted to give some of that trust back.

"You said you'd changed since high school, and I was just wondering why."

"It has to do with God."

"Okay."

"You didn't seem too enthusiastic to talk about Him earlier, so I didn't want you caught off guard."

"I wouldn't ask you to change your story to make me comfortable. My story certainly makes some people uncomfortable, but you haven't walked away from that yet. From me."

"So in college I was flunking out. I was still the guy you knew back then..."

"Lots of interested girls?"

"Yeah, that." That was one way to put it. "A lot of people called me a player. That wasn't really right, though. I'd stay with a girl while it was fun and easy, but as soon as the relationship got deeper or difficult, I'd bolt. *Dysfunctional* is probably a better word than *player*." He sighed. This was nothing to be proud of, and it was hard to talk about now. Embarrassing. But Elsie deserved to know all of him. "And I was drinking too much, too. One morning in my midtwenties, after years of partying too hard, I woke up with a headache, like usual, in someone else's room, and I barely recognized the girl when I woke up. It's like something just clicked then, like God finally got my attention. I realized I didn't want to live like that. It was so meaningless, all of it. I'd been taught that God had a purpose for my life and I decided I wanted to find that and that it wasn't one woman after another and alcohol. So I quit all of that. I went back to school and got my degree, then moved back home to fly for people like the Troopers. I may start a flight-seeing business one day, show people around the state, but right now I like feeling like I can help people while using the skills I have."

"Like me." Elsie smiled, and he could see it, even in the dark. The moon fell on her face, illuminating them a little. Wyatt hoped the trees hid them enough from anyone walking by.

"Yeah. I'm not sure how much I've been able to help…"

"Plenty." She cut him off. "I can't imagine being here alone."

"In the woods or on this island?"

"This island." She went quiet for a minute, and Wyatt

didn't know what she was thinking. He did notice the way she was still beautiful under all this stress.

"So...when God gives someone a second chance like that..."

"I like how you put that," he broke in, and she smiled.

"Thanks. When God does that, is it like half a chance, though?"

"What do you mean?"

"Like he doesn't totally forgive you, right?"

"He does. The Bible is really clear that when we ask for forgiveness, He gives it to us."

"So you have an entirely fresh start."

"Yeah."

She was frowning. "You don't act like you believe it, though."

"What do you mean?"

"I don't know. You just don't seem to act like someone who knows it's all been erased."

"I believe it." Even as he said the words, though, Wyatt understood why she wouldn't have known his beliefs by his actions. "You don't believe forgiveness is possible?"

"I don't know what I believe. You and Lindsay make faith seem so real. Lindsay always has, and listening to you talk now, it'd be ridiculous not to think that sounds appealing. But ever since you told me you'd changed... I don't know. You seem so careful now. Are you sure *you* know God has forgiven you?"

Wyatt would have said yes. Obviously he knew that God forgave and gave second chances, but maybe Elsie was right that he hadn't forgiven himself, and that maybe he didn't fully acknowledge the fact that God had fully forgiven him. He was still thinking when she hit him with the last question he'd have expected.

"So… Do you have a girlfriend now?"

"No." He answered quickly, though Elsie was pretty sure she'd caught him off guard. "No girlfriend."

"Why?"

She'd noticed how determined he was not to flirt or give the impression he was interested in her. He was overly careful now and she hadn't put her finger on why that bothered her until this conversation. How did someone have faith that God was real and would forgive them for the wrong they'd done if they didn't actually live like it? Elsie had a full life. She didn't need faith as some kind of add-on. If she were to have faith, it would need to be something real, something real that actually mattered.

"You know what?" Elsie started talking again. "Ignore the why question. That was too much. Sorry, Wyatt." She laughed and heard how nervous it sounded. They were alone in the woods and she was scared, so she'd walked them into conversational dynamite so they'd have something to focus on other than the dead body lying somewhat nearby.

"I'm never going to deserve a girl like…the kind of girl I would fall for now."

His voice was huskier than it had been a minute ago, wasn't it? Or was that just Elsie's imagination?

"I don't think that's true," she said quietly, almost surprised at herself that the words had left her lips. His eyes were on hers now, asking questions she didn't know if she was ready to answer. She didn't know if she *had* answers for them.

Her phone vibrated just as she was wondering if she was brave enough to follow this line of conversation any further.

"It's Trooper Richardson. We're on our way to you and didn't want to alarm you. We just landed on the island and a team is heading up to you."

"Thanks. I appreciate you letting me know."

"We've got a crime scene team to process everything there, and a pilot ready to take you home."

"Thanks." She slid the phone back into her pocket and told Wyatt what they'd said.

When the troopers arrived at the scene, Elsie briefed them as best she could and then Trooper Richardson confirmed for her that they could leave. If the troopers had any more questions, they would call her.

She swayed a little and Wyatt reached for her hand to steady her. She took it, noticing again the impact that small touch had. They started walking away, still vigilant for any threat. But the way the sky was slowly starting to get light again was giving Elsie a chance to relax slightly.

Which only allowed her more time to think.

The investigation was out of her hands, the missing person dead, the threatening stranger gone for now. What was on her mind now was Wyatt.

That was it, just…Wyatt.

The way he was so selfless to help other people, the way he was a natural protector, all of it appealed to her.

Could he ever…feel the same way about her?

She wasn't brave enough to ask. Not really. Was she?

"You said earlier you didn't deserve the kind of woman you'd fall for now."

"Yeah?"

"What if…? What if that wasn't true? What if you did find someone?"

Her heart was pounding in her chest now. Her timing was all wrong, but Elsie had never been great at relationships. Every moment that had passed in the last twenty-four hours had made her feel like she was on a collision course for Wyatt, her teenage crush morphing into something that exhilarated her and terrified her.

He didn't answer. Just stopped walking and looked over at her.

Elsie couldn't breathe. What did she want him to do, to say? It wasn't like she was trying to flirt with him here in the woods. She'd never been good at flirting.

But she really did wonder. What if he found someone? And if it wasn't her, would she be okay with that? Would it be enough for her to know that, one day, she might figure out how not to be alone, too?

She was afraid it wasn't.

"I'd still wish I'd lived differently. I would still think she deserved better."

The way he met her eyes, his gaze steady and unflinching, made her think she wasn't alone in her feelings. But while she was willing to take the risk…Wyatt wasn't. Maybe it wasn't selfish; it sounded like he was more worried about the risk he would be to *her*.

But it was still a no.

Elsie nodded slowly, moment past, not sure she'd ever be brave enough to broach the subject again.

"When we get back to town," Wyatt started, "you need to get some sleep."

"I'm the one who fell asleep during my watch," she said, voice wry, "which implies that you're the one behind on sleep here."

"You need it more than I do. I'm worried about you."

Worried about her heart…presumably, if she'd read the situation right and he was sort of talking about her. Worried about her sleep. Worried about her safety.

"I'm not that fragile, Wyatt. I can handle some rough days."

"But you shouldn't have to."

What could she say to that? It was sweet that he felt that way, but something still worried the back of her mind, that if she were one of his friends he viewed as "strong," whether they were male or female, would he worry less? Why didn't he see her as strong?

They'd discussed too many heavy subjects over the past twenty-four hours, and much as she wanted to fight about it, Elsie did know she needed sleep, so she decided to leave that conversation alone.

The rest of the walk to the beach was made in silence, Elsie watching Willow closely for any signs of trouble and seeing none. Her heart felt like a weight this morning, her job more like a sentence than a calling.

Next time. She'd do better next time, put Willow in the right place so she'd be more likely to see success. Lists of things she could change ran through her mind even as a voice in her head reminded her that no matter how well she did "next time," it wouldn't fix it for this woman she'd been searching for and failed to find before it was too late.

There was an airplane waiting for them on the beach, manned by a pilot whom Wyatt greeted by name, which made Elsie feel better. Without much conversation, they boarded the plane and took off back to Destruction Point.

Looking out the window at the blues, greens and the browns that late summer was starting to show in patches, Alaska's subtle giving-in to fall, Elsie still felt overwhelmed by the past couple of days. She was left with too many questions, the resolution insufficient to give her any measure of closure.

"You okay?" Wyatt asked, looking at her with concern in his eyes, but she didn't want to talk in front of their pilot, so she just nodded. They could talk later.

Or maybe they'd return to town and go back to being exactly what they'd been before. Polite near strangers who sometimes saw each other at holidays.

Somehow, that made her as sad as anything else had today. Tired or not, Elsie vowed that the moment they reached town and she could get herself back to her cabin, she'd crawl into bed and go to sleep. She'd lock the doors and take precautions, of course, but she had to sleep. And at least that way she wouldn't have to think.

ELEVEN

The ringing of her phone startled Elsie, who had been sitting at her small kitchen table, attempting to eat… breakfast? Lunch? It had been six in the morning when they'd arrived back in town, and she'd had a granola bar. Now it was ten and she was eating some ramen noodles she'd heated on the stove.

She reached for the phone, not knowing if she wanted it to be Wyatt or not. Her thoughts were all tangled up there. She hoped it might be Lindsay. It might be time to talk to her friend about…everything.

Unknown number. Hesitating for only a second, she answered. "Hello?"

"This is Trooper Richardson. I need to talk to you about the case. Are you alone?"

"Uh…yes. What's going on?"

"The victim was not Noelle Mason."

"What?" Questions flooded her mind. "So who was our missing person? How did we get the wrong victim profile?"

"I'm not explaining well. Noelle Mason *is* our missing person, and as far as we know, she's still missing. The dead woman is someone else."

Then Elsie hadn't failed. Not yet, anyway. She was sitting in a warm kitchen, in dry clothes, eating a bowl of ramen noodles, while someone she could have the power to find was in the woods, possibly in danger. She shoved her chair back.

"Tell me more," she said as she went to gather her gear.

"Preliminary investigation says the deceased is Rebecca Reyes."

"Wait—the woman who was hiking with Noelle Mason in the first place? She's the one who made the missing-person call. Did she go back to search for her friend without telling anyone?"

"It's too early to say. I'll admit it is unusual, but the troopers are looking into it."

Elsie could take a hint that she'd pried as far as she was going to be able to. As a K-9 SAR worker, law enforcement sometimes kept her in the loop, as much as ethics would allow. And sometimes she never heard another word about a case she'd worked, except what she could read in the newspaper, the same as anyone else. Switching focus, she said, "I have to find Noelle. If the attacker is still on the island…"

"Given the experience you had last night and the danger you were in, a decision was made to pull you from this search and ask another K-9 and handler to fly in."

Her breath caught in her throat, her chest tightening. Rationally, she understood that another team could do the job. It didn't *have* to be her and Willow looking. What mattered was finding the victim, not who found her.

It still stung and she took a deep breath and the trooper continued.

"But no one is available, no one with the experience needed to work this kind of terrain, with a dog who is trained in both human remains and live search tactics."

His phrasing of the second part wasn't quite right, but Elsie knew what he meant. She had a scent dog who could work with overall scent, or trailing a particular scent, as *well* as being able to find the missing person if the worst happened and they were not alive.

"So it's me and Willow?"

"If you're still willing. I should mention... Not all my coworkers think anyone should be out here. It's clear someone dangerous was on the island, possibly still is. They're investigating for any signs of other planes or boats, and we are considering it dangerous. It's a massive risk you'd be taking."

She took a deep breath. No one else was available. Which meant they couldn't take her off the case if she told them the information she'd been withholding. Information that law enforcement needed now. "Trooper Richardson, there's something else you need to know. I was attacked in my house four nights ago. The man knew my name and said something about my past and finding me. I heard the same voice on the island the day I was shot at, and again after Wyatt's plane was set on fire. I wanted to find Noelle and not be taken off the case, which is why I didn't say anything. I should have and I'm sorry. I would very much like to search if you're still willing to have me."

The hesitation on the other end of the line confirmed all her worst fears and Elsie almost wished she'd kept quiet. But not quite, because if people's lives were at stake, she had to do anything she could to give law enforcement any information they could use.

"Thank you for telling me," he finally said.

"Can I stay on this search?"

"Are you still willing? Especially if there's a personal connection like you're saying…"

"Still willing."

"We'll send a plane as soon as possible."

"Thank you. I'll be on it."

She hung the phone up, adrenaline already pumping through her. The nap she'd gotten would have to be enough. That and the strong instant coffee she planned to add to her supplies in her backpack.

As she packed, she glanced once or twice at her phone on the table. It seemed to mock her with its presence.

Should she call Wyatt?

He'd want to know. He'd made the search better and she'd needed him, if she was honest, but… At the end of the day, this wasn't his fight, no matter how much he was willing to make it that. And with his concussion, he wouldn't be her pilot. Could she bring a regular civilian untrained in SAR work on a search when there wasn't a solid reason for him to be there?

This was where a little more sleep might have come in handy, easing her tangled mind and helping her to make better decisions, but right now Elsie didn't think calling him was the right thing to do.

She loaded herself and Willow into her boat, prepared for yet another trip over to town. This week of back-and-forth boat trips was almost enough to make her wonder what it would be like to live in town. Instead she fought with the wind as it tossed her hair in her face while she pulled up anchor and readied the boat, then fought with the waves as she drove the boat toward the town docks.

After disembarking, she found her eye drawn to the slip where Wyatt kept his boat. It was there, which was what she'd expected. Of course he would be home, probably with a malamute glued to his side. He'd texted once this morning about the dog apparently missing his company, and sent a picture of his face smooshed against Sven's fluffy brown face. He'd told her Lindsay had been feeding him while he'd been gone working with her so much, but apparently it wasn't the same to Sven as having his owner home.

The text seemed to indicate that he wanted to keep being friends, and Elsie thought that was probably better than nothing... But she needed time. She still felt raw from all they'd been through together, then just abruptly separating as they had.

The small local airport looked the same as it had when she'd last boarded Wyatt's plane. Had that only been yesterday morning? She still hated that his plane had been another casualty of this case. She didn't feel right about him losing something on her behalf.

He'd have said she didn't force him to help, that he'd wanted to and it was all worth it to him. How could a man say things like that and still define himself by the utter jerk he had been in his past? Clearly Wyatt had changed.

And clearly he wasn't ever going to leave her mind alone, since she was standing here looking around to find her pilot, thinking of what he would say.

Wait.

Was that Wyatt over by that airplane talking to someone?

They were the only ones at the airport, at least that she could see, so heart beating faster, Elsie walked in their direction.

The expression on Wyatt's face was enough to stop her cold, or would have been if she'd been a weaker woman. He was angry, that much was obvious. And maybe…hurt?

"You didn't tell me you were heading out again." He didn't sound like he'd slept at all.

"I almost called." It was all she could offer.

From the shake of his head, Elsie knew it wasn't good enough.

"Elsie Montgomery?" The other pilot stuck his hand out for her to shake. "Mike Wallace, SeaAir. I'll be taking you out to the island today."

"Despite the fact that the wind changed and conditions aren't favorable for flying in that area?" Wyatt asked.

"I think we'll hit a window."

His bravado was forced—even Elsie could tell that. Mike Wallace looked to be about twenty, and while she didn't doubt that a younger man could be a good pilot, how many hours of experience *did* he have? Was Wyatt just being overprotective or was there really good reason not to fly today?

"Could you give us just a minute?" Elsie said to the pilot in a voice that was sweet and gave no evidence of what she'd experienced in the last several days.

The kid nodded once and climbed back into his plane.

"What are you thinking?" she snapped, turning to Wyatt. The sweetness was gone, her voice more biting. As short as she was, she was a force to be reckoned with when she was angry.

"I was thinking you're not a lot of help to anyone if you're in a plane at the bottom of the Gulf of Alaska. I was thinking you'd have enough sense to call me so you wouldn't be out there alone."

"Oh, so now I don't have any sense?"

Wyatt blew out a breath, raked a hand through his hair. "Don't be like that."

"What are you trying to say, then?"

"Please don't go," he finally said, after a long moment of silence. "I don't think it's safe."

"Noelle is still out there, Wyatt. The woman we have been looking for wasn't the one who was killed. She's in danger from the elements, lack of food, lack of water, even with the creek on the island…"

"And from someone trying to kill her."

"Yes, exactly!" Elsie sounded triumphant.

Wyatt shook his head. "Exactly. They're still out there and for some reason they are after you, too."

"Maybe just because I'm searching for the missing woman?"

"You don't believe that for a second. Neither do I."

They stared at each other, Wyatt trying to keep his breathing calm. She was her own woman, an adult who had been making her own decisions and choices for longer than he could imagine. But right now, Wyatt was sure he was right about the weather. This wasn't a safe flight.

"I'm not asking you to stop searching."

Her mouth opened and her face looked shocked he would even have said something like that, so he quickly started to shake his head, holding up his hand to stop her.

"I know I don't have any right to ask you to stop. But please, for today, listen to me."

She stared at him for a moment, then pulled out her phone. He stayed quiet. Waited.

"Officer Richardson? This is Elsie Montgomery. I very much want the search and I understand the necessity of hurrying, but I have a friend who is concerned about the weather right now...The pilot thinks there will be a window...Yeah. Right. I do understand that... Yes, exactly. I suppose I agree, and we will plan on that. Thank you."

She looked up at him. "He's going to check the weather and make a call. Either send a more experienced pilot now or send me with this one when it's cleared up a bit."

"Let me come with you." He hadn't planned to ask, much less sound desperate like that, but the words came tumbling out before he could stop them.

"Really?"

"I want to help. I know I can't fly you, but..."

"Let me think about it." She seemed to consider him. "For now, want to go to the police station? I've got a friend there who will let me use their resources."

He stared at her.

She shrugged. "Sometimes it's necessary to help me with missing-persons cases. She only lets me access things I'm allowed to. We could look up other missing-persons cases around here. Maybe something will help me see how to search better, or where to start in a way that will break this loose."

It was better than not being invited along anywhere, so Wyatt nodded, eager to do something. "Yes, definitely."

Neither of them said much on the short walk. Destruction Point was so small that Wyatt rarely drove in town. He wished they had the privacy of a car now, though. He had so many questions to ask her. He waited until they were in a basement room in the police department.

"So why do you think someone else was on the island? And is this connected to you and the guy who seems to be after you?"

Elsie shook her head. "I don't know how any of that works, to be honest. I…" She trailed off, then turned to face him fully. "I finally told a trooper this morning about the intruder."

"And they're still okay with you heading up the search?"

She nodded.

"I don't like it."

"You don't have to. I don't, either. But I don't think I have a choice. I'm not safe anywhere, and at least if I'm out searching, I'm doing some good." She let out a breath, looked at the stack of cases her friend had printed out for them of missing people in the area.

"Do you want to look through this half and then we can switch?" She looked over at him and Wyatt found himself nodding. He was starting to suspect there wasn't much this woman couldn't convince him to agree to.

Why did the one woman who had sparked something inside him back to life—something familiar but

so much different, purer, *fuller*—have to be a woman
who felt like she should be off-limits?

As he flipped through the pages in the folder Elsie
had given him, he found himself surprised at the sheer
number of people who had gone missing in the general
area of the island where they'd been searching. The reasons were as varied as the people, but there had been
many who had disappeared over the years.

He read until his eyes stung and was just about to
suggest taking a break when Elsie spoke.

"I need food and coffee if I'm going to keep this up."
She paused, seeming to consider her next words. "Want
to take these printouts back to my cabin?"

At least that would give him the break he needed
before he lost all ability to read and process visually.

"That sounds good. You don't mind the company?"

"No, I'd rather you be there than be by myself anyway." She hesitated. "Being alone isn't quite the same
as it was before, you know?" It was the closest she'd
come to admitting that the incidents of the last week
had impacted her at all.

Wyatt was determined more than ever not to leave
her to face this on her own. If only he could convince
her to let him go with her to the island. He didn't want
her to have to be alone anymore.

TWELVE

Elsie had intended to get straight back to work after they returned to her cabin, but after the time they'd spent in the police department conference room reading through case after case, her eyes and heart needed a break. Too many people did not get found. Her job reminded her every day that she'd been lucky to not be lost on that island until hunger or exposure had overtaken her.

So instead of diving back in immediately, she found herself stalling. It wasn't like being on the ground in an active search. She *hoped* that the time spent poring over these cases would be time well spent, whether they saw something that helped her approach a search differently or, even better, found a connection somehow between an old case and her current one. Anything that helped focus their energies so that when she and Willow did get back to the island they had a more targeted area to search would be helpful.

"Do you, uh…? Do you want anything to eat? I mean, I don't have anything super interesting, but I've got sandwich stuff."

"A sandwich would be great." He smiled appreciatively, and then Elsie watched as he sank to the floor beside Willow and started to rub the dog all over. Willow, usually a bit standoffish around people who weren't Elsie, rolled entirely onto her back, seeming to soak in the attention.

If she hadn't already liked him, seeing him sitting on the floor with her dog certainly would have been enough to catch her eye. That was the problem with Wyatt. He was so much more than she expected, and she never seemed to be able to anticipate the ways he would be attractive to her. He just *was*.

"Here you go." She handed him the sandwich and sank down onto the couch, grabbing a handful of chips from an open bag. She ate in silence, then looked over at Wyatt. "Those files depress me."

"Seeing all the people you couldn't help?"

She sighed and nodded.

"Which ones stuck out to you so far? Anything give you new ideas for how to search like you were hoping for?"

"This one…" She tugged a couple of pieces of paper out of a manila folder.

"A man wandered off hiking in the Caribou Hills and never came back?"

"Yes. I picked it just because it's close to here. And because searchers found him by examining his life and patterns and analyzing how he was most likely to move and then following that path. That's something I didn't do enough of in the previous days of searching. I need to get to know our missing person better, guess how she thinks, get inside her head." She reached for another example, handed it over to Wyatt, who skimmed it as he ate his sandwich. "Here's another."

"Boater who disappeared not far from here... Ever found?"

She shook her head. "Just the boat. I helped with that case, but we were never able to find him. Not alive or dead. It just catches my eye because it's one of my failures."

"Do you think of them that way, really? Like, do you carry them around like that?"

She scooted to the floor so she was sitting beside him on the other side of Willow, who was still stretched out, enjoying the attention he was giving her.

"I don't know. I don't mean to. But probably. It makes the wins sweeter, though..."

Elsie frowned, then stood up.

"Elsie? Where are you going?"

"Give me a second..." Her mind was spinning, something in what she had thought or said turning the wheels of her mind in a way that was confusing and clarifying all at the same time. Wins...

"Why did someone start coming after me now?" she muttered as she dug through the piles that had accumulated on her small table in the last couple of days.

There it was, the newspaper article from the successful rescue that had taken place only days earlier...two days before the threat against her had surfaced? No, only one. The rescue itself had taken place one day, the article had come out the next, and that night someone had broken into her cabin.

"What if someone...?" It was too strange to voice

aloud the thoughts formulating in her mind, so Elsie paused and went back to the file. Pulled out another case.

"Here." She handed it to Wyatt, who looked it over. She sat back down beside him.

"Three-year-old found…island… Wait—this is…"

"Yes. It's me."

She waited for his reaction, anxiety and excitement building within her, and she started to wonder more and more if she was right. "I know I said this earlier, but I can't get it out of my head. What if someone wanted me dead? Like, what if it wasn't just child neglect or abandonment? My whole life I assumed no one wanted me. Like I was forgotten there and not worth going back for or something."

He recoiled like she had hit him.

Elsie held up a hand to stop him before he even started. "I know it bothers you that I would think that way, but you need to let it be. You can't do anything to change all of that. What I'm wondering is… What if I was wrong? What if someone actively wanted to get rid of me?"

"Like murder instead of neglect? Like you really did witness a crime?"

He put into words what she could not, but she still flinched a little at the word *murder*. It seemed so harsh, but in reality, leaving a three-year-old on an island, even without such stated intentions, was just as cruel.

"Yes," Elsie said even as she hoped it wasn't true. Who would want that in their past?

She pulled her phone out and started googling. If different memories kept appearing when she was on the island, triggered by smells or sounds, would it be possible to trigger memories herself?

Every angle she could try to search, she did so. *Murdered women* and then the year. *Alaskan women murdered. Domestic violence Alaska.*

Nothing.

"One more idea…" she mumbled. Elsie typed in the phone number for the Office of Children's Services and asked around until she found someone who could pull up her old file.

"Is there anything in my file," she asked, hoping desperately that her one last attempt to trigger some kind of flashback wouldn't be a failure, "that points to domestic violence or violence of any kind?"

If the woman on the other end of the phone thought it was a strange question, she didn't say so. She just told Elsie she was looking.

"No… There's really just not enough detail…" The woman stopped. "Maybe one thing."

Elsie definitely believed in leaps at this point. "I'd love to hear anyway. I can't tell you how much I appreciate your help."

Across from her, Wyatt had looked up from the files and was watching her, though she knew he could only hear her end of the conversation.

"There's a note that you kept repeating 'Mommy crying.' No mentions of violence specifically, but…"

"Thank you for the help," Elsie said even as a chill ran down her arms. She hung up the phone.

Crying.

The darkness. No, not just darkness. The hall closet. Hidden behind the coats. Screaming. Crying. Her mother.

Her mother had been crying. The woman in the dream was her mother.

Breaths coming rapidly now, Elsie nodded. "It fits." She swallowed hard against the emotion building, tears threatening to fall even as her throat stung. "I think someone wanted to get rid of me—murder me—" she stumbled over the word again "—because the flashback... there's more to it and...I think they killed my mother and...I was there."

"Oh, Elsie."

He reached for her and Elsie was surprised at how easy and natural it felt to be in his arms. The longer he held her, the more she felt herself relaxing into him and the more what had started as a hug of reassurance moved, at least for her, into a deep awareness of how close she was to Wyatt.

And how much it could take her mind off even the darkest elements of her past.

He pulled away, his face a muddle of emotion.

It was a lot to take in, Elsie realized, even for someone who, well, wasn't her. Wyatt looked stunned, and she'd, of course, not delivered any of those thoughts as graciously as she could have because she was still stumbling through explanations and guesses herself.

"Even reading this..." He trailed off as he waved the packet she'd handed him about her rescue. "And you saying you didn't think anyone wanted you..."

"When I was a kid," she felt the need to clarify, as she definitely didn't need his pity.

But he was already shaking his head. "You act that way now, living out here without people nearby, refusing the help of law enforcement that first night. Refusing my help initially."

"Really? I'm the one who lives like they're not wanted?" Elsie said defensively.

"What is that supposed to mean?" Wyatt's voice was calm, so calm. Low. Serious.

"Maybe it's good that you're not a player anymore, but now you act like…like…like no one would want you."

"That's completely different."

"How?"

"'Cause I'm not you. You're different. You deserve better."

"And you don't?"

They were facing each other now, sitting on the floor.

"We aren't talking about me."

"Maybe not then, but we are now." She'd told herself she wouldn't be so bold again, not after how awkward that last conversation had been, but something had snapped inside her when he'd shown such care and concern, trying to convince her she wasn't unwanted. As though that wasn't just the most ironic thing she'd ever heard.

His eyes were fixed on hers, and he was sitting inches away. She had the sudden desire to…to reach over and pull him closer…maybe to kiss him.

Yes. That was exactly what she wanted, if she was honest with herself. For days she had watched as he proved he had changed.

She believed in that change, but he didn't. He didn't see himself the way she did.

Wyatt Chandler was never going to start something

with her. Earlier she'd have said it was because he didn't want that, and now…

Maybe it was because he felt like he didn't deserve it. Or maybe he was just scared.

Either way, Elsie could control very little in her life right now. But she *could* control this.

Before she could stop herself, she moved closer, her breaths growing shallower the closer she came, her lips parting, eyes flicking to his mouth. Then his eyes.

He knew what she was doing.

He didn't stop her.

The whisper-soft brush of Elsie's lips across his, followed by a second kiss with more intensity but not less gentleness, didn't catch Wyatt off guard, but nor would he say he was prepared for it.

This was what he'd wanted for days, what he'd tried to stop himself from dreaming about since he started to see Elsie differently. Wyatt didn't know why he hadn't paid attention to Lindsay's friend back then, but he'd noticed now.

Just as slowly as she'd begun it, she ended the kiss, pulling back just enough that they weren't touching, but lingering close to him for a moment longer. He could freeze time right there. Forget about finding redemption and proving himself. Forget about murder investigations and stalkers.

"Wyatt?"

Her voice was soft and hesitant. Much more hesitant than her kiss, which had been confident. Unwavering.

"Yeah?"

"Are you sorry I kissed you?"

She was so honest, so willing to drag conversations into the light. She was missing the self-protective instinct to hide her feelings, or maybe she simply didn't play games.

All Wyatt had done as a kid was play games.

He wanted to be different now. Wasn't completely sure if he knew how.

Help me, God, he prayed, meaning it as much as he'd ever meant any prayer. He couldn't return her honesty with anything but the same.

"No, Elsie. I'm not sorry." He should be. Shouldn't he?

Shame. Guilt. Peace. Forgiveness.

He was overwhelmed.

"I just…" He moved back slightly, ran a hand through his hair. "I need a second."

She backed up. "Take a second. It's fine. As many seconds as you need."

Was it hot inside her cabin? Wyatt needed space. Air. Away from Elsie, even though at the moment all he could think of was how he wanted to pull her back toward him, kiss her until he forgot all about who he used to be and until she knew how much he cared about her.

But wouldn't that make him who he used to be?

"I need… I'm just going to step out…" He stood, moved toward the door. "Just for a second."

Her eyes were wide. Clear. Questioning, maybe. He hated that she wondered how he was feeling right now, but as much as he'd like to reassure her, he was so entirely overwhelmed that he couldn't put any of it into words. "Lock the door behind me."

"I will," she promised, and he stepped out into the cool, damp air.

Wyatt walked into the woods, realizing another reason Elsie might want to live out here. You could have all the space to think you wanted when you lived on the edge of the woods like this.

For years all Wyatt had wanted was to convince people that he had changed, to get them to believe him. Now Elsie did believe him, but it was somehow still overwhelming to him.

God, I don't get this. I'm trying to get better, to be a different kind of man.

Sure, he hadn't been to church, he didn't pray too often. Surely God would rather he wait until he'd proved himself. Until he had *really* changed.

As quick as the thought came, Wyatt knew it was wrong. Without thinking, he looked up at the sky. Blinked. Was that God, correcting him without a word?

The truth that he'd learned as a kid, he remembered now standing in the woods, was that God wanted His people to know Him. To talk to Him. Not to wait until they were some impossible version of perfect that they would never be.

I'm sorry, God. I shouldn't have stayed away. The list of things that would have been easier to handle if he'd taken them to God first seemed to run through his mind all at once.

God... Wyatt started walking again as he prayed. *About Elsie. What do I do? It would be so easy to fall in love with her, but what do I know about love?*

Again, almost as soon as he had the thought, the moment the prayer had left his heart, there was an answer. Verses from the book of 1 Corinthians in the Bible came into his mind. "Love is patient...love is kind..."

Okay, so God had spelled out some things about love. He could work on those. He could show her differently that he loved her, not just with words that could be empty, not just with kisses that could be motivated by something besides love.

Not that the kiss they'd shared had been like that. Wyatt was sure he'd never felt a kiss with so much genuine emotion in it. Elsie kissed softly, but with her entire heart. It seemed to fit with who she was as a person. Gentle. Sweet. But strong.

He had told her the truth. He didn't regret the fact that she'd kissed him. Was it possible for them to start a real relationship? When this was over and Elsie didn't have to keep looking over her shoulder, would she still be interested in him?

"I think I'm falling for Elsie," he whispered to himself, to God, to the silence of the woods.

Elsie.

The woods were quiet. So quiet, and a sense of discomfort crept over him, causing him to tense his muscles. He shouldn't have left her. He'd been gone too long already.

Wyatt started back toward the cabin, reminding himself that no one liked to be smothered, and Elsie had been living on her own for years before now without any trouble at all.

The cabin in the distance looked the same. The warm glow of light coming from the windows reminded him of Elsie herself. Everything was fine. He'd overreacted.

He hurried to the front door of the cabin, pushed it open.

The kitchen looked the same. The living room looked

the same. His eyes were drawn to the spot in front of her couch where they'd been sitting on the floor beside Willow when Elsie had kissed him.

But Willow wasn't there.

Elsie wasn't there.

Everything was so very quiet.

"Elsie?"

She wouldn't have left after that, would she? He'd told her that he'd be right back, but what if she hadn't listened? She could have gone looking for him.

He had to find her. Shutting the door behind him, Wyatt hurried back into the woods.

"Elsie!" The woods that had felt so welcoming only minutes before now seemed to have darkened, become somehow malevolent. If Elsie had been taken out of the cabin against her will, she could be hurt, or worse. He'd seen no sign of blood, but that didn't mean very much.

He hoped Willow was with her, though he almost wished she was with him so they could find Elsie together.

Come on, help me. He prayed to God, desperate and with no other plans for finding her. Wyatt knew it was a long shot, but he had no idea what else to do other than search.

God would have to work out the rest.

THIRTEEN

Pain in her face almost blinded Elsie, causing her to squint as she was pulled through the woods, barely keeping her feet underneath her. She'd fought her attacker at first, refused to go with him. But the man in the ski mask had slapped her full across her face. The throbbing pain made her realize it was better to go along with him than continue to be hurt.

Willow. Where was Willow? She'd heard her growling earlier but hadn't heard her recently.

"Quit that." The roughened voice, muffled by the fabric of the ski mask, was indistinct and full of hatred. "You've caused me enough trouble. Didn't I tell you to stop running?"

She started fighting again out of instinct, arms flailing, hoping she connected with the man in some way. He grabbed a handful of hair, and Elsie cried out in pain. Would Wyatt hear? How far could he have possibly gotten? She hadn't yelled up until now, didn't want to remind the attacker that she could call for help, lest he gag her. It seemed wiser to wait and only yell for help if she knew someone was actually close enough to hear.

But pain had made holding back nearly impossible. Would it help? She didn't know.

"Shut. Up," the man growled in her direction, yanking again at her hair, and this time Elsie kept her mouth shut. Barely.

It was hard to guess at the distance they'd gone, figuring in being dragged, but it hadn't been many minutes after Wyatt had left that the man had opened the door of her cabin.

She forced her eyes open a little and tried to get her bearings.

"Elsie!"

Her heart flooded with relief and she closed her eyes and almost involuntarily whispered "thank you," though she didn't know if she was trying to talk to God or just speaking her thoughts aloud.

Before she could think anything else, the pressure on her hair was released. She stumbled back in time to see Wyatt's fist connecting with her attacker's jaw.

A growl and a flash of white and she saw Willow out of the corner of her eye launch herself toward the man. Her good dog had been trailing them all this time, waiting for the right moment to save her.

"Willow, come." Elsie said the words firmly, not wanting her to be in Wyatt's way and accidentally get one of them hurt.

Willow seemed indignant to have been taken out of the fight, but she obeyed and ran to Elsie's side. Elsie watched as the two men continued to fight. She was fairly certain Wyatt was winning.

Finally there was no doubt. Wyatt had the other man pinned to the ground.

"Call the Troopers," he said to her, panting from exertion.

"I don't have my cell phone. It's in the cabin."

He nodded, pulled his out and tossed it in her direction. She scooped it up and made the call, quickly relaying their situation and location.

"Someone is on the way," the dispatcher said.

Elsie hung up, then wondered briefly if she should have stayed on the line. Her gaze fell back on the man Wyatt had pinned.

"Who are you?" Elsie asked. Seeing him like this, she realized he wasn't a mysterious voice in the woods anymore. He was a real human, just as defeatable as anyone.

Still, he must have wanted to maintain some level of power, because he wouldn't answer her. Even after Wyatt yanked off the ski mask, he said nothing. She didn't see anything remarkable about his features that would help her to identify him.

Worse yet, he didn't look much older than she was. Which meant that he would have been too young to have been involved in what had happened to her all those years ago.

"You're working for someone, right?" Wyatt asked, and Elsie waited to hear if the guy said anything.

Still, he stubbornly refused to talk.

Frustration rose within her, pressing on her temples. She wanted to make him answer but knew there was nothing she could do. She hated being powerless.

The troopers appeared faster than she'd hoped, breaking the strange tableau of Wyatt holding down the masked man, Elsie and Willow watching in silence.

* * *

They hauled the man away, and Elsie and Wyatt were alone.

"You're okay?" she asked him, her voice quiet.

"Yeah. He doesn't punch that hard."

"Still." There was so much she could say. He was still very possibly a murderer, if he'd been the one responsible for Rebecca Reyes's death.

"I can't believe I left you alone." His voice was anguished. There was no other way to describe it.

"I'm okay."

"I should never have left you. What if…?"

"Nothing happened," Elsie insisted, then hesitated and reached up to rub her head, which still burned. "I mean, he hurt my head when he yanked my hair. And my arm is pretty bruised, but I think it's all right. I'm fine overall."

"I still shouldn't have left."

"Did your walk…" She trailed off. "…help at all?"

"I don't want to see you hurt."

"I told you I'm fine—"

"I don't want to see you hurt by *me*."

She stared. "Why would you hurt me?"

"I…I think I'm falling in love with you, Elsie." His voice was steady, his face serious.

Elsie's heart fluttered.

"I think it might be mutual," she whispered back, leaning a little closer to him before stopping.

This time, Wyatt was the one who initiated the kiss, and it was gentle, slow and curious, his lips moving against hers carefully. *Cherished.* That was the word for how she felt right now.

When he broke away, Elsie wasn't ready for it to end.

"We have to get back inside. Just in case that's not the only guy after you."

The worry in his tone was very real, but somehow his concern made her smile. "I'm okay. You don't have to be so worried about me." She meant it in multiple ways but he shrugged it off.

"Please? For me?"

If it was that important to him, she would go inside. There was no reason to make him worry unnecessarily.

At least, not yet. Because Elsie still needed to pack. The clouds were breaking up overhead, glimpses of blue showing in the sky.

This might be her chance to get back to the island and find Noelle Mason. Hopefully still alive.

And with the way things had changed over the course of this day, she might let Wyatt come with her. He'd probably worry less that way.

As they made their way through the woods back to the cabin, Elsie tried to write his concern off as paranoia. But no matter how much she tried, she knew that she'd come close to being killed several times. And one detail was still bothering her about this last attack.

The man hadn't killed her in her cabin. He'd been hired to take her…somewhere.

But where? Why?

And who was behind it all, pulling the strings?

Chills chased down Elsie's spine and her earlier confidence was replaced by a sense of deep foreboding and pressing anxiety. Somehow, she felt like she was close to finding out the answers to her questions. But how would they be answered? And what would happen to her if they ever were? Those were questions that haunted her.

Wyatt was right to be worried.

Because no matter how much she might want to pretend otherwise, Elsie was still not safe.

Elsie had immediately started repacking her gear when they'd arrived at her cabin, and given the fact that the weather looked like it was clearing, Wyatt had stopped trying to argue with her about her desire to go back to the island to search.

He hoped she found Noelle alive. Hoped she got her answers about her own past, and that she could live with them. The stories she'd told him were difficult to process even for him, who hadn't been there. He couldn't imagine how she would deal with any truths her past might hold for her.

Especially when she didn't know God, didn't have faith in Him to help carry her through. *God, help her to know You.* He hesitated over the second part of the prayer. *Whatever it takes.* As much as he wanted her safe, well and happy, Wyatt knew that she was none of those things if she didn't know Jesus.

He thought about what he wanted, for everything to work out. Bad guys? Gone. Elsie? Safe. The two of them…dating? Dating Elsie in the traditional sense of how people usually dated would seem weird somehow. She was too special for something like that. No, if they ever made the world safe for her again, he'd pursue her heart, be her friend, fall in love with her a little more every day and then for the rest of his life if she'd let him. He prayed.

Within the hour they were back in the air.

"You wish you were flying, huh?" Elsie sent him a sympathetic smile and Wyatt shrugged.

"At least my head injury wasn't worse. And I appreciate that you waited until I thought it was safe."

"You know a lot more about flying than I do."

She wasn't wrong. Wyatt just grinned, shrugged a little. Elsie smiled back.

So much had changed in the last few hours. Despite the danger and the fear, having Wyatt with her was like a dream come true. A dream she hadn't even known she'd harbored. She'd always assumed that she would be alone. It had been how she'd lived most of her life and she'd never let herself wonder what it would be like to depend on someone else.

Wyatt himself was unexpected, but incredible. He'd grown so much from the handsome, unattainable boy of her teenage crush.

Wyatt reached for her hand, and she enjoyed the feeling of his warm fingers wrapped around hers. Now it was time to focus on finding Noelle.

All the way to the airport, they'd worked out a plan. There was another beach on the island, more remote, on the other side. They'd always landed at the main beach, where most hikers had boats or planes drop them off, so this time they'd start at the other.

There were two reasons for this. First, Elsie wanted the element of surprise. Whoever was after her might expect them to continue using the main beach, so there was a chance they'd arrive undetected.

Second, they'd come up empty too many times. Willow would find a trail and then it would go cold. She wasn't sure if it would do any good, but Elsie hoped that changing the location where they started their search would help.

"You ready?" Wyatt looked at her and Elsie felt her confidence grow. All of the stress of the last few days had focused within her, giving her the drive to finish this search.

She could feel it. They were going to find this woman. Today.

"I'm ready." Beside her, Willow's eyes flashed. Today, they were both as ready as they could be.

Still, Wyatt looked uneasy. She laid a hand over his. "Don't worry."

Wyatt's smile didn't reach his eyes, but he was trying. She'd give him that.

The plane descended toward the island, the ocean seeming to rise to meet them. Her heart skipped a beat or two. It was time. No more planning. No more wondering if her new approach to the search would be successful.

As the plane touched down on the ocean waves, Elsie took a deep breath. The start of a search was sometimes chaos. Coordinates. Points last seen. Victim profile. The noise could get overwhelming, but then when the work started for the day, when it was her and her dog in the woods, everything was quiet. Fully focused.

It was time.

They grabbed their packs and climbed out of the small plane. As they organized their gear, the pilot took off again. He would be back for them in six hours, if all went according to plan.

"All right, boss. What do you want me to do?" he asked.

She took a deep breath, put her shoulders back. "Much will be the same as last time. Keep an eye out, have my back. We are looking for areas where a person with only casual wilderness skills would go." She'd finally made more of a profile and thought that Noelle would likely have taken more established trails. They'd spent time the last few days walking through thicker woods, and while Willow had been able to catch the scent several times, she'd lost it also.

This new approach was going to help. Elsie was sure of it. She felt bolder, too, with the knowledge that whoever had been after her was possibly out of the picture. Even if, as they suspected, the man had been hired muscle, hopefully whoever was actually after her would not have had time to regroup. Everything was lining up for them this time. "Let's go," she said to Wyatt, taking a deep breath and heading to the woods in front of them.

Where the other side of the island boasted a trail that gradually led up, this one began with an immediate, drastic climb. It was steep enough in places that Elsie started to second-guess herself and wonder if Willow was going to be hindered in her movement, but her dog exceeded her expectations once again. Elsie reached up to get a grip on the rocky edge of the steep face they were climbing, needing three points of contact here where the rock was slick and wet.

"You okay?" Wyatt called from behind her.

"I'm good." This was far from the most difficult terrain she'd covered.

Following Willow, they made their way upward until

they'd reached the top of a ridgeline. The island below unfolded before them, woods thicker in some places than others, so many variations of green almost overwhelming Elsie's eyes in their vibrancy. This spot provided a lookout of the entire island.

· One of the most common decisions people made was to get to a good vantage point where they could see. Up here, Elsie felt organized, committed to her plan.

Had Noelle then gotten lost after she'd been here, or had someone intercepted her?

"Where would she be now?" she whispered aloud.

"What was that?" Wyatt asked.

Elsie shook her head. "If someone took her, where would they have gone? Are they even still on the island?"

Thinking like a lost person was one thing; it was an integral part of her job. But thinking like a criminal... She wasn't used to that.

"It would depend on why she was taken," Wyatt pointed out.

"All right, Willow. I'm flying blind here." She bent down to her dog, who came forward to meet her. Rubbing the soft fur of her face, Elsie leaned forward until her forehead was resting on her dog's head, both of them sitting in stillness. Refocusing.

"You've got this, right?" she whispered.

Willow seemed to nudge her, that deep, inexplicable understanding that some dogs had with their owners.

"What's the plan?" Wyatt asked her as she stood.

She shook her head slowly, took a deep breath. "This is Willow's time to shine. She's got it, I'm sure she does."

FOURTEEN

As Elsie and Willow walked back and forth along the ridgeline, Wyatt followed them. This didn't make a lot of sense to him, wandering in a way that felt aimless, but he trusted Elsie.

And she seemed certain that Noelle had been up here at one point. Because she suspected it or because the dog smelled her? He wasn't sure.

She seemed now to be searching for the scent. It was fun to watch the excitement on Elsie's face as she worked in tandem with her dog, weaving in and out of trees, into bushes, all around.

There was no doubt she was determined, approaching this search with a new fire that Wyatt admired and found extremely attractive. She didn't quit, ever. She was heart and perseverance in a small package. He'd underestimated her once, he knew. But he was trying not to do that anymore. The fact that she was so capable was one of the things he admired about her.

"Wyatt!"

He turned quickly. So lost in his thoughts she'd gotten behind him. His chest pounded with his heartbeat.

But no, she was right there and she was smiling. Nothing bad had happened.

"She's got it! She's got the scent again." Another grin, wide across her whole face, and she motioned for him to follow.

Seeing her now, he could imagine how she'd survived here as a toddler. Where some people might wander through the woods, Elsie was *part* of the woods. She didn't seem daunted by obstacles or roots in the trail. She swung around trees almost as fast as Willow darted around them. He was out of breath keeping up, and he wasn't in bad shape.

They wound down the ridge into a valley in the heart of the island, the vegetation growing thicker here in the shade. Devil's club, with its intimidating spikes on the stem, seemed to grow all over, and Wyatt did his best to avoid the broad leaves, which would make a person itch something terrible if he managed to brush against them.

It was cooler in the shade, and the entire atmosphere felt so different from at the top of the ridge. Up there he'd been able to see, and he'd caught a bit of Elsie's excitement.

Down here amid the overwhelming growth of the shadowy forest, he felt a sense of discomfort.

Just a small one. He looked at Willow. The dog showed no evidence of noticing anything was wrong. He must be imagining it.

Wyatt glanced behind him, quickly so that he didn't lose sight of Elsie in front of him for long. No sign of anyone.

Writing it off as paranoia, he kept going, following them down the narrow pathway and around a corner.

He almost ran straight into Elsie, who had stopped. "She's here."

He looked around. "Alive?"

Elsie didn't answer.

"Elsie?"

"I don't know. Willow... I don't know."

He had no idea what that meant, how alerts worked. Was there a difference in the alert for a living person versus a dead one? Willow was patiently sitting, looking back at Elsie with confidence in her face, near an especially thick stand of devil's club.

"I'll go." He moved forward, but Elsie put out a hand to stop him.

"No. This is my search, my dog."

"But you're taking an unnecessary risk. You don't *know* she's the person under there."

"She's who I told Willow to look for. I trust my dog, Wyatt. Trust *me*."

He just wanted to keep her safe. But he *did* trust her. He nodded.

She moved forward, carefully, and Wyatt bent low to get the best view into the thickness of leaves.

He could see someone's feet and legs. The person was lying on the ground. Dead or alive, he still couldn't tell.

"Noelle?" Elsie asked.

A low moan answered. Wyatt held his breath and waited.

It was almost impossible to see into the stand. Whether the victim had chosen this as a hiding place or the attacker had tried to stash her here, Elsie could understand why.

It didn't appear any bad actors were around the area. Willow seemed alert, having found her target, but not uncomfortable or anxious. Elsie meant what she'd said to Wyatt. She had to trust her dog. And she did.

She crawled forward on her knees, doing her best not to rub against the leaves. She'd found with devil's club, moving slowly often prevented one from being injured by the delicate poisonous hairs on the leaves or by the giant spikes on the main stem from which the plant got its name.

"Are you okay? I'm search and rescue. We are here to help." She reached for Noelle, who was still lying on the ground. She'd moaned once but now made no noises.

The woman stirred. From where she was now, Elsie could see her entire body. Her eyes were closed, and she had a small amount of dried blood on her face and shirt.

Assessing her as best she could for broken bones or other injuries, and feeling fairly confident there was nothing majorly wrong, Elsie grabbed the woman's lower leg and gently shook it in case she was asleep.

Another moan and the woman's eyes opened. Fear flashed in them.

"No, you're okay, you're okay," she immediately started to reassure her, but the fear didn't leave Noelle's eyes.

"Who are you?"

"I'm search and rescue. My dog found you and we are going to get you off this island."

The woman started to sob, though it was more sound than tears. Elsie guessed she was extremely dehydrated. She offered the woman a bottle of water and trail mix, which she consumed slowly.

There would be time for questions when they were off the island. As many things as Elsie wanted to ask, she knew they should wait.

She crawled backward, stood and turned to Wyatt. "We need to get her out of here."

He glanced at his watch. "Still three hours until the plane is supposed to come back. I'll call for a helicopter. They'll be able to get her out faster." He stepped away and she heard him talking quietly.

Pride in her dog swelled in her heart. Not only had they found her, but in only three hours of searching today. *Alive.*

Noelle, making crying sounds again, looked up at Elsie. "Rebecca," she croaked. "My friend, we were hiking together. We got separated. I don't know how exactly..." She trailed off.

"Why were you here?" Wyatt asked from behind.

Noelle started and Elsie sent Wyatt a small glare.

"He's with me," she explained, shaking her head slightly so he'd know not to chime in anymore.

Elsie helped Noelle out of the bushes, and the other woman stood, dusted herself off, seeming to regain enough composure to talk.

"I was here on a hike. With Rebecca." She frowned at them both. "That was how it started, anyway. I should have known..." She trailed off, eyes starting to widen again. "Rebecca and I lost track of each other. I think after someone tried to kill me? I don't know. I didn't see the person who shot at me." She looked at them, terrified. "Is Rebecca okay?"

This time Wyatt didn't answer, but looked to Elsie, who considered her next option.

"She's dead," Elsie said gently. "I'm sorry."

"He killed her." Noelle was crying again.

"Who?" Elsie held her breath. Did Noelle know the killer?

Her face paled. "I don't know."

Did she really not know or was she just not saying? It was hard to distinguish between a trauma response, genuine ignorance of a situation, and someone who was simply too scared to talk.

She looked to Wyatt, knowing he understood people well. He seemed to understand what she was asking, but he just shook his head slowly. He couldn't get a read on her, either.

"When should the helicopter be here?" she turned to Wyatt and asked.

"Within the hour. They'll land at the beach where we were today." He kept his voice low. Because he was trying not to alarm Noelle? Or because he was trying not to be overheard?

"We need to go. Are you okay to walk?"

Noelle nodded and the three of them started to make their way back up the mountain toward the ridge.

They managed to walk at a fairly fast clip, and Elsie's heartbeat pounded in her ears. She wasn't law enforcement. She'd done all that she needed to do.

The police would work on figuring out who was responsible for hunting Noelle and killing Rebecca Reyes. Elsie didn't need to get involved.

Except she *was* involved. If there was a connection to the people who had been after her, she needed to figure out who they were and why they were pursuing her.

Once they were over the ridge and back to the beach,

the helicopter was waiting for them. She turned to the woman, knowing this might be her last chance to talk to her.

"I need to know who was after you."

For a long moment, Noelle said nothing. Elsie waited.

"I think… This is going to sound paranoid. But I worked with someone…" She hesitated. "Travis Cattleman."

Elsie frowned. Why did that sound familiar?

"The senator?" Wyatt asked, and that pinged Elsie's memory.

"Yes," Noelle confirmed, looking uneasy. "He's the one who suggested this place to me. He said he'd hiked it."

"Did you see him here on the island?"

Noelle shook her head. "No. The person who attacked me wore a ski mask, but…he didn't seem familiar."

Elsie could feel Wyatt's eyes on her and she could imagine the kinds of questions he had.

"You'll probably have to tell all this to the police, too." Wyatt spoke up.

Noelle frowned. "Can't you just pass it on to them?"

"We aren't law enforcement," Elsie explained.

"Then why did you want to know all of that? Why the concern about who had been after me? Isn't that something the police should be asking?"

"Hopefully they will," Elsie said. "But we are looking into things, too…trying to get a picture of what's going on."

"Why?"

Elsie wondered how to say this. When she finally

spoke, it was with confidence. "We're looking for another missing person, too."

"Someone tied to this case?" She frowned and Elsie nodded slowly. "Who?"

Elsie took a deep breath. "Me."

They'd climbed into the helicopter just after Elsie's revelation to Noelle. None of them said anything the entire ride back to Destruction Point. They'd no sooner gotten out of the airplane than police met them.

"Thank you for finding her," one of the Destruction Point police officers said to Elsie.

"I'm glad we could."

"You're definitely a one-of-a-kind team." A trooper spoke up. "Not many people would have walked into that kind of danger. Usually we prefer to send a trooper with the K-9 team as backup. I'm sorry we weren't able to today, but you did fantastic."

Elsie's smile was thin and watery. Wyatt could tell the praise made her uncomfortable but wasn't sure if it was because she didn't like to be singled out and given accolades, or if it was because she didn't feel like she'd earned the praise and felt guilty because she'd concealed her possible connection to the case.

"Thank you."

"At least the senator can't try to hurt her again, if he really was behind this," one of them said as they started to walk away, ready to take Noelle back to the city to continue hearing her testimony of what had happened and to return her to her home.

Elsie frowned. "How can you be sure?"

The trooper pulled out his smartphone and thumbed

at it before showing her a newspaper headline. "Didn't you hear? His plane went down. He died this morning."

Wyatt and Elsie shared startled looks.

"Where?" Wyatt asked, not surprised a plane had had trouble, given the bad weather that morning, but somewhat surprised that it could really all be wrapped up this easily.

"Not far from here, near Fisherman's Cove, during that foggy period of time this morning. That's why manpower was low today."

He was more thankful than ever that Elsie had listened to him and not insisted on flying out in weather that wasn't appropriate for someone who was not instrument rated to fly in.

Elsie seemed to understand what he was thinking, because she turned to him and offered a smile.

"I'm glad she will be safe now," Elsie said.

The trooper nodded. "We are, too."

And Wyatt? He was glad that if the same person was after Elsie, then she would be safe as well. The rest was just icing on the cake.

After watching law enforcement fly away, Elsie and Wyatt started walking back toward town, to the docks, like they'd both agreed on it.

"You don't have to follow me there anymore," Elsie said with a small smile. "I think it's safe now."

Safe. That word had never sounded quite so incredible as it did to him now. That was what he wanted Elsie to be for the rest of her life. Safe.

"I'll follow you home anyway if that's okay. I won't stay," he hurried to say. "I know you've got to be sick of me by now."

"Not at all." Her face was entirely serious, her eyes meeting his unflinchingly.

His eyes dipped to her lips, which she curved into a soft smile.

"I think you should come over. We can eat and celebrate the fact that this is over."

He still couldn't quite believe it, but she was right. After what, three, four intense days? They were done with this particular case.

But resolution didn't feel quite like he'd expected it to. Probably because they hadn't gotten as much resolution as he might have hoped.

"Do you know if the police are going to pursue a motive in all of this?"

She shrugged. "They don't tend to tell me much. What they said tonight is more than they usually say in a case I help with."

"But this is different. You're involved personally. And you said you told them what you knew?"

Elsie nodded. "Yeah, but how are they supposed to tie me in? I don't have a name. I don't have a past. All I may ever know is that I was somehow connected to this, but you know what? That's fine. I just want it over. In the past. That's all."

Wyatt nodded slowly. "But you'd like to know."

"I'd like to know as far as it relates to me," she admitted as they approached their boats.

"Ironic, though, isn't it?" she continued with a small smile. "I wanted to know about my past. I wanted to know who would have something against me. I know that now, sort of, assuming the person who died in this crash was the one who was after me as well… But I still don't have any more answers as to why they came after me, or who I was."

Her smile was sad. The lack of resolution made the celebration feel hollow.

But they still had plenty to be thankful for, Wyatt thought. He wrapped an arm around her and pulled her in for a hug. She folded into his chest, small and fragile against him. He held her carefully.

After a minute, he pulled away. "Ready for me to walk you home? By boat, that is?"

She smiled at his attempt at humor and nodded.

"Yeah. I would like that a lot."

Elsie hadn't been to town in a bit longer than she'd remembered, so rather than a grand celebration feast, they shared part of a box of Cheez-Its, some beef jerky, celery and an apple. But Elsie didn't remember when she'd been happier. Her and Wyatt. Who would have guessed?

Part of her was still terrified. Not because of Wyatt—he'd proved himself trustworthy over and over during this case. He cared about her more than Elsie could ever remember anyone caring, but...

Didn't that give him the power to hurt her? And could he really love her if her past always stayed a secret? Would he know who she was if she didn't fully know?

Or did she not need to know about her past to fully know herself?

The questions plagued Elsie. She was exhausted, physically and emotionally, but it had been worth it to find what looked to be the start of a relationship she would never have seen coming.

A fresh wave of optimism hit her. Maybe she would never know who she had been, but you didn't need to know your entire past before you could pursue your future. Wyatt was the future. Watching him, talking to him, wishing he would press his lips to hers again...

"What are you thinking over there?" he asked from his place on the couch beside her.

Elsie shrugged. "Just thinking about you."

"Me, too, about you." They rested in silence for a moment longer.

Then she said, "But...I'm also thinking about who was behind these attacks. Do you really think a senator would hire a contract killer?"

"Travis Cattleman. Sounds like a fake name." Wyatt made a face.

She snorted. "Do you think maybe I was in the way of his career somehow? I mean, think about it. I was three when someone tried to make me disappear the first time."

He immediately seemed to understand what she was implying. "Just the right age to be the proverbial skeleton in someone's closet."

"Or maybe it was some kind of political power move. Maybe I'm related to someone who opposed him and it was revenge? Or I was supposed to be a bargaining chip?"

"Any of those make sense."

It hurt that they would never know. Maybe she was just supposed to learn to live with uncertainty. Was that what she was supposed to have learned from this entire situation?

"I wish you could have found out."

Even though she hadn't put it into words, Wyatt understood. He saw her feelings and considered them in a way no one else ever had.

She looked over at him, nerves jumping in her stomach. What now where Wyatt was concerned? He'd said he was falling in love with her, but that had been during high stress, out of their real world. What about now? Would he feel differently back in town, with their lives and jobs always crowding in and likely reminding them how different they were?

Nerves humming, she angled herself to face him a little more. "Thank you for caring."

"You make it easy to."

"Should we play cards? Go for a walk?" Elsie laughed self-consciously. "I'm not really used to having visitors."

"I just want to be here with you," he said, his voice deep, his eyes steady.

"I could get used to you being here for me," she admitted.

She saw something spark in his eyes as he heard her words.

Then Wyatt slid from the couch.

Got down on one knee.

Panic rose in her chest.

"Elsie, would you marry me?"

She stared, as a roar in her ears intensified. What… was he doing? Proposing? Really? Now?

"Wyatt, stop, no. Get up."

"I love you."

"You don't even know me! Get. Up!"

She was yelling now, and Elsie hated herself for it, but what had he been thinking? One second everything had seemed perfect and now…it felt like it was falling apart. Why did this happen to her? More importantly, why had she thought that she, a person who was used to being alone, could change and be anything but alone for the rest of her life?

FIFTEEN

She was pulling away. That was all Wyatt could think as he felt the ache in his knees, stood from his impulsive kneeling position and then sat back down on the couch.

That wasn't how he had envisioned this at all. Wyatt had messed up. He knew it as surely as he knew his own name. After all this time of being patient, waiting to fall in love till he'd found the right person, he'd rushed once that had happened. Elsie was right for him. He was convinced of that.

"I, um." He cleared his throat, wishing he could fast-forward through the awkwardness. "I'm sorry about that, I guess?"

"Don't…apologize." She stood up, started to walk around the room. Her eyebrows were scrunched together in a way he found adorable. "You just don't even know me, Wyatt."

He bristled. "Yeah, I think I do."

She shook her head. "It's been what, a week?"

"We've known each other for decades."

"We've known *of* each other," she corrected him. "It's not the same thing."

"What else is there to know, after everything we've been through together?"

At the moment, her expression didn't indicate any kind of positive emotion toward him. But hadn't they been kissing less than ten minutes ago? Had she told him she was falling for him, too?

Wyatt wanted to leave. The desire revealed something about his nature he didn't particularly like. The old him walked away when things got difficult, and he didn't want to be that guy. He wanted to be the kind of guy who could stick around through everything and work it out.

Besides, last time he'd left Elsie's house to process alone, she'd ended up being dragged through the woods. While the threat against her appeared to be gone, he still wasn't willing to take the risk.

She'd been choosing her words carefully. She said, "There's so much more to someone than you can learn in just a few days. I want to be really known like that, not just have someone know a little bit about me and be attracted to me."

Of course she did. He heard what she wasn't saying. Her entire life she'd wanted someone to really know her, and who she was, and he'd messed up.

"I'm sorry. I can't take the proposal back."

She stopped pacing. "I think you need to go."

His heart dropped. "Don't, please. Let's talk about it. I don't want to run away from you, Elsie."

Her eyes betrayed no emotion, but she was shaking her head. "Just go."

It was the last thing Wyatt wanted to do. But he was

trying to be a gentleman. She'd told him twice now, so he didn't feel like he had a choice.

Breathing a quick prayer for her safety, and for God to do something with the mess he'd made of things, he opened her door, then shut it behind him.

Why couldn't he have asked her on a date? Or told her she was beautiful? Or given her chocolate or a puppy? *Anything* to show his growing affection that wasn't a proposal would have been better. He saw that now.

Wyatt exhaled deeply, squeezed his eyes shut.

And wondered if she'd ever give him—give *them*— a second chance.

It was strange, the way she almost felt like they'd come full circle. Elsie was in her bed again, sleepy but sleepless, unable to rest. Just like she had been before everything had happened. The man who broke into her house, the new search...Wyatt...

What had she done?

Earlier, she had been so sure that her decision had been the right one. It was better to chase Wyatt away if he didn't really know her than to risk him becoming disappointed when he realized she wasn't what he thought, right?

Apparently not right, because Elsie was miserable. Willow was annoyed with her and had already moved from her comfy spot on the end of the bed, where she'd been curled up on the blanket that usually stayed folded at the end, down to the floor, where Elsie's restlessness wouldn't wake her.

Night had finally fallen in the woods, the dim sky outside her bedroom a beautiful shade of twilight blue.

She hadn't shut her curtains tonight, and she could see the dark silhouettes of the spruce trees that surrounded her cabin.

Everything was peaceful, as it should be. Willow showed no evidence that any sense of danger was anywhere nearby.

This wasn't at all related to her safety or to the events of the last few weeks. This was only related to Wyatt Chandler. The man whose heart she'd stomped on earlier.

And what about her own heart? Her life alone had been fine. Actually, it had been lovely. She loved being out in the woods, the freedom she had as a single woman to decide when she came and went, the way she was able to pursue her job. Yet she missed Wyatt.

The man himself, for who he really was.

Was it possible she could have been wrong? Did he know her better than she'd thought? Maybe there could be a way to fix this.

Morning would be the ideal time to figure that out. Surely she could go to his house, apologize, explain…

Then what? She still didn't think the proposal was a good idea. But the way to change how little they knew each other was…to get to know each other. They could do that.

He'd said he loved her, and she did believe him. And then she'd sent him away, angry.

Probably no matter how much she tried to sleep tonight, she was going to keep chasing this thought, like a butterfly she could see but never catch, always off in the distance just out of reach. Her brain just wouldn't stop, trying to work this out, which to her truly seemed unfixable.

She gave up on sleep somewhere in the middle of the night, before the light had started to come back, just at the darkest point, and grabbed her light jacket.

Willow looked up at her, eyebrows rising.

"I have to talk to him," she told the dog. "I think I'm falling in love with him, too. I think it scared me. I think..." She heard her voice waver, felt the lump in her own throat grow. "I think maybe I don't know how to do this."

Willow stood, walked toward her.

"You're coming, too, huh? Wouldn't dream of leaving you."

This was it, Elsie thought as she pulled on her boots and locked the door of the cabin behind her. She stood outside for a second, letting her eyes acclimate to the dimness. The moon was bright enough there was no need for a flashlight, but the shadows outside did take some getting used to. At least now there was no need to startle at the shadows. Troopers were investigating the cause of the plane crash, but if all their suspicions had been correct, she should be safe now.

She felt safe, too, all the way to her boat and across the bay. The ocean was calm tonight, accepting, it seemed, of her desire for safe passage to town, not fighting her in the least.

Was that what it would be like when she talked to Wyatt? Would everything go more smoothly when she stopped fighting against her feelings and her anxiety about not being in control, about not being sure whether or not she'd be any good at being in a relationship?

They'd both been right last night, Elsie thought. She'd said he didn't know her well and he didn't. But maybe Wyatt had been right, too, that he knew her anyway.

She wouldn't know for sure until she could talk to him, see his eyes. She was ready to take a leap of faith, to take a risk. But she wanted to talk to Wyatt first. Even now her heart was hesitant. Afraid.

Elsie hated being afraid.

She docked the boat at Destruction Point's marina. Remembering where Wyatt's house was, she walked toward it, Willow trotting along beside her.

When she reached his house, it was dark. Not surprising, as it was late. But...Wyatt's front door was wide open.

Her heartbeat started to pound in her chest, fear seemed to weight her legs, but she propelled herself forward anyway, wishing she had some kind of weapon with her, just in case someone was waiting for her, someone who wasn't Wyatt.

Eyeing the door, practically willing Wyatt to walk out of it unharmed, Elsie pulled her phone from her pocket and dialed 911.

"Wyatt Chandler's house has been broken into. His front door was left open and I'm afraid someone took him."

"Location, please?"

"I don't know his address." Frantic, she looked around for the 911 numbers that even a small community like Destruction Point had. She finally found them, on the side of the mailbox, and read them aloud to the dispatcher. She quickly filled the dispatcher in about Wyatt's last known whereabouts.

"We'll be there within five minutes."

"I'm search and rescue," Elsie said. "My dog and I are on the way to find him now."

Elsie hung up. Five minutes.

She hurried inside the house. "Wyatt?" The first room, a living room connected to a small kitchen, was empty. It was neat, with very little evidence he'd even been home.

The next room was an office, with papers and folders everywhere, but still fairly neat. No one had ransacked this place. They weren't searching for anything and, Elsie thought, they didn't seem angry. This felt more intentional.

Chills chased down her spine. Was it a trap? For her?

Wyatt would tell her to go home, that the risk wasn't worth it, but as her search continued to reveal too little as to his whereabouts, Elsie started to feel more and more strongly that to leave was exactly what she couldn't do. Not now. If Wyatt was in trouble, then it was because of her. She couldn't abandon him now when he'd been so determined not to leave her alone with all of her troubles. She could feel the tension in Willow building as the two of them walked through the house together.

There was one more room she and Willow still hadn't searched. His bedroom door was closed and Elsie felt like she was violating his privacy by going in there, but at the same time, she didn't have a choice but to search it, too.

She reached for the door. Knocked. "Wyatt?"

No reply, but she did hear something. A scuffling. At her feet, Willow whined.

She knocked again. "Wyatt?"

When there was still nothing, she eased the door open. Willow charged in, a blur of brown moved toward them, and before she could react, Elsie saw Willow, her bright white fur pouncing around the room with a brown malamute mix that she knew had to be Sven, Wyatt's dog. He dwarfed Willow, but he seemed friendly, though obviously disturbed.

"You okay, bud?"

Elsie reached to pet the dog, then started to look around the room. Maybe Sven was the world's friendliest dog, a definite possibility, but he acted as though he hadn't seen anyone in hours. She searched the room, and not finding any clues, she shut the dog back in the bedroom.

Strange he would have been shut in there, rather than in the nice kennel she'd seen in the living room. That one was a brand she'd long envied but hadn't quite gotten to spending money on yet. It didn't make sense that Wyatt would have left the dog closed up in the room.

The intruder, then? That made more sense.

Where were his food and water bowls?

Finally, she found them in a little nook off the kitchen, near a storage closet, which she checked and found empty of anything alarming.

The food bowl was empty. That much, she'd expected. A dog didn't get to the size Sven was without a healthy love of food.

The water bowl surprised her. Dry. Entirely. Elsie filled both bowls, her heart pounding as she put the pieces together.

If Wyatt had come home, he'd have taken care of his dog.

The door was open. But was it possible someone had come here to find Wyatt and discovered he wasn't home? Then…what?

Waited for him?

Elsie texted Lindsay, asking if she knew where her brother was. Her friend answered almost immediately. She did not.

Anxiety flooded through her. As though she didn't already feel awful enough about the way they'd left things last night, now she could imagine him leaving her cabin, walking through the woods…getting attacked where? His boat was gone, but she hadn't looked in town to see if it was in its regular slip.

He could be anywhere.

And the police would be here any minute, and if she got caught up in talking to them, her opportunity to try to find him using Willow to search would be gone.

She scrawled a note on a paper towel, explained that Wyatt might be in danger due to the events they'd been investigating, and wrote her phone number. They could call her later.

Right now? She had someone to find.

Wyatt's head throbbed, the thrum of pain the first thing he noticed when he regained consciousness. He remembered leaving Elsie's, remembered their fight, and then things started to get blurred in his mind, the throbbing somehow hammering away at his memory.

Elsie was safe… Wasn't she? As far as he remem-

bered, she was, though that was no great reassurance
with as questionable as his memory seemed right now.

He sat up, noting the crushing of spruce boughs
underneath him. He was somewhere on the forest floor
and the sky told him it was the middle of the night.
There was enough light that he'd be able to find his
way around without a flashlight, but not so much that
he could see anything very well.

No one approached when he sat up, though Wyatt
didn't know if that was because he'd succeeded in moving quietly, or because no one was here waiting for him
to wake up.

He rubbed his forehead, wishing he had access to
pain medicine. It was difficult to think against the pain.
Everything felt more difficult, and thoughts didn't come
as quickly as he felt they should. Once again, he tried
to make his mind cooperate, and to walk through what
he remembered.

Taking a deep breath, then letting it out, he tried to
get his bearings. In the distance he heard…something.
Voices?

He crept forward, toward the voices, hoping for some
kind of hint as to where he was. The landscape was
generic to the general corner of Alaska where he was
from. Dark brown dirt and rocky ground. Salty air from
the ocean. Dark spruce trees towering overhead.

Hopefully he was still within walking distance of
Elsie's cabin, except… His boat. They hadn't taken his
boat, had they?

As he approached the voices, and studied the area up
ahead of him, he discovered that the voices were in a

clearing on the edge of the land, at the top of what appeared to be a cliff that fell away to the ocean.

Had no one been left to guard him? Was it because the landscape was inhospitable enough that they assumed that would keep him still? A cliff in front of him, mountain behind him… Why was he important to them, anyway?

"…kill him…?"

That…did not sound good.

"Will her dog be able to find him?"

"She'll come. She found the dead woman, right? The one who was asking too many questions?"

"True… I just don't want to drag this out any more. With the election coming up, I have too much to do. You and Reynolds should have been able to handle this. Then he…arrested…"

As he'd feared, he was being used as bait. Whoever these men were—they were men's voices—they were setting up a trap for Elsie.

God, don't let them get her.

He couldn't let her be caught because of him.

He rubbed his forehead, trying to form a plan. If he was the one in danger, he could just run deeper into the woods. Evading the men who'd attacked him would be his main priority. But Willow would be able to find him no matter how well he hid himself, and the longer it took for her and Elsie to find him, the more they'd be in danger.

So maybe he was stuck here. At least until he could figure out where *here* was and how to get out.

His eye caught something past the men. A flash of

white. He crept closer so he had a better view through the thick trees. There, on the shore, they had his boat.

If he could make it there, he'd have transportation.

"Don't even think about it."

The voice was low and gravelly, and before Wyatt could turn, pain exploded in his head again and everything went dark.

Guilt was Elsie's companion as she ran through town with Willow, taking back streets and wooded patches of forest until she was at the docks.

As she had feared, Wyatt's boat wasn't in his slip. And she definitely hadn't seen it by her dock, which likely meant someone had snatched him after he left her cabin. The wilderness around where she lived was vast and she'd only explored parts of it, but Elsie knew that was where she and Willow would go now.

The fact that Wyatt was likely being used as bait did not escape her. But what else could she do? Law enforcement needed to be involved, which was why she'd called them, but there was no way they'd be able to find him as quickly as she and Willow could. He'd already sustained a head injury within the past couple of days and Elsie shuddered to think of what they'd have done to him in order to get him under their power. She knew there was no way he'd have gone willingly.

She knew a lot about him for only having gotten to know him this week, Elsie realized. Enough that, really, she could see some of Wyatt's points. Just because she'd have preferred he wait before broaching a subject like marriage didn't mean he'd been thoughtless in his proposal. He'd rushed, majorly. Half of her wondered if it came from his desire to give her the chance to be part of a family. She didn't know. All she really knew was that she'd have liked to have been asked to date him, not marry him.

Still, he'd made himself vulnerable and she hadn't been sensitive to that at all. Elsie had messed up, too. Big-time. Now he was gone and she couldn't even tell him she was sorry.

"We have to find him, Willow," she said to the dog as they climbed into the boat. "We just have to."

The ocean had grown moody from the peaceful state it had been in earlier. The swells were unpredictable and larger than usual. Elsie held the wheel, kept her gaze fixed straight ahead and headed toward the point where her cabin sat. This was Wyatt's point last seen, she was almost sure of it, so this was where they would start the search.

They pulled up onto the beach and anchored without incident, and Elsie climbed out of the boat, then ran inside her cabin to grab her backpack of supplies and a thicker jacket, as the morning air was chilled and the ocean spray had dampened her clothes and hair.

"Ready, girl?" she asked her dog, strapping Willow's vest on and holding out an old T-shirt of Wyatt's that she'd grabbed out of what she guessed was his laundry pile beside his bedroom door.

Willow got the scent and stopped, meeting Elsie's eyes.

Trust her dog. She had to trust her dog.

Wyatt was relying on her. She'd already let him down last night, when she'd refused to listen to him and had shut him out instead. She couldn't let him down again.

SIXTEEN

Willow had caught Wyatt's scent in the air immediately, which had encouraged Elsie, but hours had passed and they were venturing deep into the mountainside woods that stood guard over her home, deeper than Elsie had ever been before.

The clouds were thick today, entirely obscuring the sun and blanketing the spruce forest in thick fog, heavy blankets rolling all the way down to where the land met the ocean.

Her phone had rung several times, but after checking it was neither Wyatt nor the local police, she hadn't wanted to stop to answer it. Not when Willow still had the scent. Now, though, she knew she needed to give Willow water and a break. The scent had been strong up until now and she would just have to hope that nothing changed after they sat for a few minutes. Taking care of her dog had to come first or Willow wasn't going to be able to successfully complete her job of finding Wyatt.

While Willow lapped up the water from the dish Elsie had put down, she downed a few sips herself and then slid her phone out of her pocket and called the number she had for Trooper Richardson.

"Hello?"

"This is Elsie Montgomery."

"Elsie. I've heard from the Destruction Point Police about you today—are you okay? Are you safe?"

"What did you hear?"

"They said you called in a missing person and then disappeared after leaving some kind of note?"

It sounded bad when he said it like that. Elsie explained about finding Wyatt's house broken into, and the reason she'd left the note in such a hurry.

"I'm not entirely surprised. Send me your coordinates and I'll send you backup."

She wasn't about to argue with him. She gave him the coordinates, relief flooding her. "Be careful," she warned him. "This might be a trap for me."

"You're referencing what you said earlier, that this may be tied to your past?"

"Yes. And I want Wyatt to walk out of this alive and he's not going to do that if whoever abducted him thinks they're not going to get what they want, which is me. And... Trooper Richardson, I need your people to catch these guys. Assuming we all make it through this, I want to be free to live my life without a shadow hanging over me, without wondering when my carefully crafted life is going to be obliterated by someone who wants me dead."

"Of course. What else can we do?"

She hesitated. "Look up the Jane Doe baby case from twenty-five years ago in Destruction Point. It's me." She glanced at Willow, who was staring up at her, looking rested. "For now, I have to go. Thank you for helping."

"You're welcome. Good luck. Backup will be on your trail soon."

She hung up the phone and started forward again, Willow leading the way. She appeared to still have the scent, much to Elsie's relief. It was always a gamble stopping in the middle of a search. Wind could shift, conditions could change and lessen the thickness of the scent in an area. They were lucky.

Willow led her deeper into the forest on the mountainside, where the sunlight didn't quite reach the forest floor even without fog. It was damp. Cool. She was glad she'd grabbed a thicker jacket and hoped Wyatt was okay wherever he was.

Willow stopped. Made an abrupt right. Sure enough, Elsie could see a slight trail that cut into the side of the mountain, rather than continuing straight up. They followed it until Willow edged farther right, like they were going down the mountain. Elsie could see evidence that someone had been brought through here, likely against their will. Maybe even dragged. There were several places that branches were broken in this direction, like someone had pressed against them too hard on the way through. Anticipation built within her. They were getting closer, and Willow hadn't lost the scent yet.

She needed a plan. Troopers as backup were fantastic, but Elsie didn't know how long it would take them to get there, and she didn't want to count on them for her safety. If she was walking herself and her dog into a dangerous situation, which she appeared to be, she wanted her own general plan.

Whoever was after her was not giving up, that much was clear. They must have decided to use Wyatt as bait to get Elsie within their sights again.

She was convinced that was also the reason Noelle

Mason had gone missing, though she hadn't worked out all the details yet. But it had been clear that the attacker she and Wyatt had caught wasn't the mastermind. He might be in jail now, but the danger wasn't past.

She took a deep breath. When she got to wherever Wyatt was, his condition would have to inform her decisions. If he was too injured, he wouldn't be able to run away. She'd have to play some of this by ear whether she wanted to or not.

But ideally, she would see Wyatt and be able to communicate with him before having to reveal herself. He'd help her, she knew, if he was able to do so. Would he still have the weapon she knew he'd had before? It didn't seem likely. She should have thought to grab one from his house, not that she was very familiar with firearms. She only owned bear spray. Nothing else had been necessary until now.

Her biggest concern at the moment was that if Willow alerted loudly, it would give away their position. She needed her to be as quiet as possible.

All of that assumed she found him and that it was soon. Elsie had no idea what to expect or where he might be. If they'd come by boat, which she expected given the fact that his boat was gone, then why did the trail lead this way?

She looked at her dog. Unless... The scent over the water might have disappeared, and the scent on the beach could have been dispersed by the wind. Was Willow actually picking her way across a mountainside to get to where the scent *was*?

Elsie didn't know anymore. She felt out of control, confused, never a good way for a handler to feel. But after all she'd endured in the last few days, she didn't feel like she could be too upset with herself. As she tracked through the trees, following her dog, she kept hoping with everything within her that they would find Wyatt.

All this time, Elsie realized, she'd been waiting to be found. She wanted to know who she really was. She'd wanted someone in her past to have missed her. It was disconcerting to know that her old identity had essentially disappeared off the planet and no one had cared. So when Wyatt proposed like that... She'd felt like maybe he didn't care about finding her, either. Not her old identity, not the story she wished she had about her past; she'd given up on that. But the woman she was now.

If he didn't know her very well now, it was partially her fault. Maybe she'd spent her whole life waiting to be found, but it turned out she was also *afraid* of being found. What if Wyatt got to know her and didn't love her anymore? It was why she'd held herself at arm's length from so many relationships.

Maybe even...why she'd held herself back from God? The now-familiar urge to pray that she'd felt so many times over the past few days was strong and difficult to ignore. The idea that knowing God meant that He knew her as well... That was terrifying to her. What if God didn't like her? Did that happen? Could someone seek out a relationship with God, admit that they wanted Him in their lives and then have Him reject them?

For the first time in a long time, she felt entirely and truly alone.

God, if You still want me, I don't want to be alone anymore. It's worth being scared, I think. I've done a lot wrong—forgive me for those things. Thank You for letting me come to You and, like Lindsay says, sending Jesus to die on the cross and pay for my sins so that I can come to You. She took a deep, long breath in. Let it back out. *I trust You, God. I'm trying really hard to, anyway, and I think that counts. Help me find Wyatt.*

Nothing changed that she could see. The woods still looked the same. The fog pressed down on them even heavier, if anything. Her circumstances did not appear to be affected in the slightest.

But she could feel a difference inside, as the flicker of faith inside her grew. Hope, that was the difference. She had hope that maybe they'd be able to pull this off. Maybe she could have a chance at happily-ever-after after all and be able to apologize to Wyatt. See if he'd let them start over again.

And finally, *finally*, she didn't feel alone.

Willow sped up her pace and Elsie took off after her. This was it. This was their chance and she wasn't going to miss it.

This time, when Wyatt awoke, he was aware of ropes rubbing against his wrists and ankles.

He hesitantly opened his eyes. His vision wasn't impaired at all. His headache? That wasn't worth focusing on, as it was worse than ever. He wasn't comfortable with the slight nausea, either, probably from the very likely concussion that he had. At least he was still in one piece.

Helpless. But in one piece.

It wasn't often he felt like he truly couldn't handle his circumstances on his own. Even when he'd come back to God, it had been with the plan to earn God's favor again, like Elsie had pointed out to him the other day, which was wrong. The truth was that he was an independent man. He liked knowing he could handle a situation.

Right now, he couldn't. He would have to trust God to see him through.

And maybe Elsie? Surely she and Willow were looking for him. He wished they weren't, since he was sure they were walking into more danger than Elsie was ready for, but he knew without them his chances were slim.

Something about the last thought caught him. Maybe that was what Elsie had meant. Rather than assume that she didn't realize this was a trap, and worry about her, treat her like something small and breakable, she wanted to be treated like the capable, brave woman she was. Maybe that was one of the areas where she felt like he didn't know her well enough.

Change was something he was used to, though. Personally, professionally. He could change, make this better. If they got a second chance.

Right now? He didn't know what to do but stay put. He could see the beach from where he was, but he was leaned up against a tree, and with his arms and legs bound, he wasn't going anywhere quickly.

"Don't even think about running," a voice told him. Not the one from earlier. That one had been rough, violent. This one was smooth and almost pleasant.

Political.

"Travis Cattleman, I assume?" Wyatt asked him.

He heard footsteps coming from around behind him, and a man came into his line of sight. Wyatt vaguely recognized him from the news. He was not quite six feet, Wyatt guessed, though it was hard to judge from the ground. Average build. Smooth, clean-shaven face. Green eyes.

Eyes startlingly like Elsie's in color, though nothing alike in their mood. Elsie's eyes sparkled with adventure, bravery. Last night he'd seen a spark of something a lot like love.

This man's eyes were calculating, exacting.

"Very astute of you to figure out." His eyebrows rose in some kind of sick amusement. "If you'd been this quick yesterday, you might not be sitting here like this."

Great, a talkative villain. Part of Wyatt wanted to roll his eyes. He hated movies where the villain monologued at the end.

On the other hand, if there was one thing he'd learned from movies like that, it was that the longer you got a guy talking, the more likely you could find some way to defeat him. This wasn't a movie, but it was worth a try. He was too helpless to do anything else right now.

"Why is Elsie in your way? She doesn't want anything to do with you."

The man recoiled. "Annie. Her name is Annie."

One question answered about Elsie's past, though Wyatt wished she were hearing it first. It didn't seem right that he would know this part of her story before she did.

"She doesn't care about you or whatever you're trying to do politically. She wouldn't have bothered you." He hesitated. "Still might not if you leave her alone." The last part was a stretch. He couldn't imagine Elsie letting this kind of injustice go unpursued, unpunished. But this man didn't know that. Didn't know her.

"Annie never had a choice. She was doomed from the start. Her mother should have…" He trailed off, though Wyatt was fairly certain he knew where the man was going. "She had no right." His fists were clenched.

"So…" His mind went to Elsie's flashbacks, to the darkness she'd described. The way she'd responded to the dying woman on the island's screams like she'd heard them before. "You killed her mother."

The fists clenched tighter, though Travis didn't say anything.

"And meant to kill Elsie when you left her on that island."

"Annie!"

Why the name mattered so much to a man who was bent on destroying the woman who had it, Wyatt didn't understand. But sometimes people didn't make sense. It was clear to him that this man, Travis, was operating under intense emotion. He'd become an even more dangerous criminal because emotional criminals were unpredictable. Loose cannons.

And here he was with a front-row seat to the madness and no way that he could think of to stop it.

"You meant to kill her," he guessed again. "But you didn't succeed, so you let her live until now."

"I didn't *let* her." The man's voice was bitter. "I *lost* her. I was so sure… I knew she'd never survive on that island. I knew I wasn't linked to her in any way. I knew it was the *best* way to get rid of her."

So that was why Elsie had gotten to live all those years.

"And then…" he prompted, not sure if the man would keep talking or explode.

"I saw an article in the newspaper. Some local fluff. My staff like to keep me informed, keep me in touch with my constituents." Wyatt rolled his eyes and hoped the man didn't notice in the growing daylight. "I knew it was her. I recognized her right away. She's like a walking version of Tressa."

Wyatt guessed Tressa must have been Elsie's mother. Was that part of the reason the man was so determined to kill her? He couldn't guess how much of the man's motivation was related to a desire to keep his other crime—killing Elsie's mother—under wraps and how much was him repeating that action. He'd been mad enough to kill the mother, whom he must have cared for on some level. Why not kill the child who he was convinced should never have lived?

"So you put a woman on that island hoping she'd be called in to find her?" That would explain Noelle Mason's presence on the island.

"She worked at a shelter I've done some work with. Publicity stuff. She and I had gotten…involved and so she was a liability anyway." He shrugged. "I knew Annie would come find her."

"But you weren't able to kill her. You killed her friend, though."

"An unfortunate bit of collateral damage. Rebecca was never supposed to die, but when she got off the island after she and Noelle were separated, she started to get suspicious about the fact that I had suggested that island hike to Noelle. Apparently she knew about mine and Noelle's relationship. I couldn't afford for her to be pointing fingers at me. So I returned her to the island," he said smoothly.

"You killed her," Wyatt broke in.

Travis continued, unfazed. "And then Annie found Noelle so fast…hence the need for the plane crash so she'd think we were out of the picture. And you… Now I can finally get rid of her."

"Leave her alone," Wyatt tried again, not needing any more of the story. "Just let her go. She doesn't care about you."

Travis kicked and pain exploded in Wyatt's shin.

"Do not tell me what to do. I have a plan. I am the one in control here, and I am calling the shots." A slow, sick grin spread across his face as he slid a shiny handgun from a holster on his hip. "Literally." He lifted the gun, aimed it at Wyatt. Waited.

Wyatt barely breathed. It took everything within him not to react. *He* knew that Willow would find him dead or alive. But it seemed this man and whoever was helping him earlier hesitated to kill him, not knowing if he would still be an effective bait. He had to use that.

"Losing patience and getting rid of your bait this fast?" He kept his voice even, the words the only provoking things. His tone was neutral.

The gun wavered. Travis spit out a curse and holstered the gun.

"When she gets here, she dies. You get to watch that. And then you'll have stopped being of use to me."

With one more kick at Wyatt's shins, the man walked back behind him, out of Wyatt's vision. He wasn't tied to the tree, so he had a little range of motion and freedom to move, but he didn't dare turn around, not now.

Right now, he would wait. He couldn't help Elsie if he was dead.

God help us. He prayed and then he started to form a plan. As he prayed, he dropped his hands to his side, hitting the lump on the edge of his pocket. His knife. How had he forgotten it earlier? There was a knife in his pocket, sharp enough to cut this rope. If he was careful…if he did this just right…

I'm going to need Your help, God. I'm never going to pull this off without You. He reached into his pocket, worked the knife out and toward his hand.

After several minutes of struggle, adjusting his position, moving his hands carefully, the knife was open on the ground. He rubbed the rope against it.

And finally, *finally*, the rope started to cut.

SEVENTEEN

There they were. Up ahead, Elsie could see two men in the trees, moving around, talking to each other. She was too far away to hear them. Willow leaned forward as though to growl and Elsie called her off. Slipped her search vest off.

She could almost feel Willow's frown. They'd gotten this close to her goal and Elsie was telling her to stop searching now?

"I'm sorry, girl. But you found him. You did well. He's here somewhere." She was sure of it. She trusted her dog, even when she couldn't see. Even when Willow hadn't given the final alert.

Was trusting God like that, too? Bigger than trusting a dog, but knowing that Someone had your back, even though you couldn't see the logic behind it?

Maybe, Elsie decided as she crept closer. Picking her way through the spruce trees, wildflowers and brush, she kept advancing until she thought she'd be close enough to hear, then crouched low to the ground and gave Willow a hand signal to do the same. The dog obeyed.

"Back for more?" She heard Wyatt's voice. The edges of it were sharp, like he was in pain or angry or both.

Either would make sense. It took her a moment to get a visual of where he was, where the voice had come from. There, beside a spruce tree, in the forest ahead of her, adjacent to the clearing where the two men were. The ocean was beyond them, but this must be part of the landscape where it dropped off in a cliff. She didn't see any kind of gradual slope to the beach, but she could hear the waves even from here. Crashing against the rocks, maybe. Her attention went back to Wyatt. Why was Wyatt just sitting there? Why wasn't he moving?

"Shut up. Keep talking and I'll shoot you now and hope that stupid dog is able to find you anyway."

Elsie rubbed Willow's ears. Stupid dog indeed. Who had tracked them across the island working from scent that had been miles away. "Good girl," Elsie whispered.

"Why kill her mother in the first place?"

"My political star was rising," the man said. Something about that voice… "If voters twenty-five years ago knew I'd had an illegitimate child, I'd never have made it out of city council, let alone to the Senate. Besides, it wasn't just that. It was that her mother—" he bit the word out "—wouldn't listen to me. If she'd done what I told her to… I assumed she had. I didn't hear from her for *years* and then I saw her. And the kid."

Elsie had to be the kid. Wait—this… Her heart seemed to catch in her throat. This angry man holding Wyatt hostage was her *father*?

Being kicked, punched, anything would have hurt less than this. She'd thought her whole life until the terror of this week that she wanted to know her past, to know her history, but to be related to a murderer…

The rest of what both men had said fully registered in her mind now.

A murderer who had killed *her mother*.

What a past. What a story.

Elsie wanted to back this one up, get out of these woods, go back to yesterday and somehow keep Wyatt safe and just live…untouched by all of this. She didn't want this.

"Killing them both made sense. But turns out the kid didn't die. Till now."

The man was determined to win. As she had suspected, Wyatt was the bait. She just hadn't understood why. All this time—this past week, anyway—she'd assumed someone wanted her dead but had never dreamed the reasons were this personal.

But this man—the missing senator?—had killed her mother. Tried and failed to kill her. This was why no one had come forward about a missing toddler, because her mother had been dead and her father had been the killer.

"I won't be your bait anymore."

It happened so quickly, Elsie almost couldn't break it all apart in her mind. But Wyatt, who she'd assumed must have been tied up, flung himself toward the man— her biological father—and the two of them were tangled on the ground. The other man rushed at them. Now it was two against one. She couldn't wait anymore.

Sprinting out of the woods, she joined the fight, hitting, kicking.

She heard one of the men yelp and realized Willow had joined in, too, and taken a bite out of someone's leg. "Willow, no."

For once the dog didn't listen, though. She must have

decided Elsie needed her help whether she liked it or not. Elsie couldn't focus on the dog because she had enough to do worrying about what was in front of her, on top of her. They were four humans in something of a pile, punching, kicking.

She took a hit to the stomach and cried out.

"Elsie!" Wyatt's voice was panicked.

"Don't worry about me."

"Aren't…you…noble." The man who'd been talking before grabbed her by the arm and pulled so hard she thought for a second he'd dislocated it.

That fast, she was out of the fight. She could hear the sounds of the continuing scuffle behind her as the other man and Wyatt fought. Their grunts and groans faded into the background and her world seemed to narrow as she looked at this man in front of her.

This was the man she'd wondered about, this man in too-new outdoor clothes, with a smirk on his face, anger in his eyes. Eyes that looked just like hers. They were related, if what he'd said was to be believed. She had her answers. She had her story. And…

She didn't need it. Once upon a time she'd have wondered more. How did her parents meet? Why didn't he want her? Why did politics matter more than his child?

Now Elsie needed none of it. Maybe she'd always been found. Maybe the ache she'd felt inside had been an awareness that she was missing God in her life, and now that she could acknowledge that He'd found her all along, she didn't need anything else. She didn't know. All she knew was that she didn't need this man.

"Not going to cry? Your mother cried."

The darkness. The closet. The screams. Elsie steeled herself against them.

"She cried because of me. She wanted to protect me." Elsie remembered now. Enough that she knew that was true. Enough that she knew when this was all over, if she lived, she'd spend some time processing these feelings with a counselor she could trust. "I'm okay, though. I'm not afraid of you."

Because God was here, God had her. And because Wyatt was somewhere nearby fighting for her.

Because in the end, good was going to win. No matter what happened to her. But... She didn't want this to be the last part of her story. She wanted that happily-ever-after. Words failed her, but she managed to whisper a *please, God* to her newly found Heavenly Father.

The man in front of her raised the gun. Aimed it at her.

Elsie closed her eyes.

The gun went off.

He was almost too late. *Almost too late.* The words echoed in Wyatt's mind even after he'd slammed against Travis, made his shot at Elsie go wide.

He'd still been fighting the other man, probably Travis's hired muscle, when he'd caught a flash of metal and realized that Travis had Elsie. He'd landed a hard punch to the man's jaw, enough to knock him out, and run at Travis with his full force. He'd thought he was going to be too late.

Maybe he had been and God had intervened somehow. He'd slammed into Travis and the shot had missed Elsie. That was all that mattered to Wyatt at the moment.

Travis screamed in frustration and Wyatt wrapped

his arms around the other man, reaching for the gun, hitting at him. But he got away. Started to run.

"Elsie, watch out!" Wyatt yelled, but this time Travis didn't go for Elsie. He just ran, attempting to evade them and escape. Wyatt ran after him.

Willow barked, joined the chase, grabbed the man by the leg. He jumped backward, away from her. Willow lowered her head. Growled and stepped toward him. He took another step back.

Too close to the cliff. Wyatt yelled, "Don't! Stop!"

But Willow lunged and Travis stumbled back and started to yell as he fell over the cliff, toward the rocks and ocean waves, and Wyatt made it to the edge just in time to see him go under and be swept out with the current.

Unlike the plane crash, this couldn't be faked. There was no coming back from this. He was gone.

Adrenaline pumping, he turned to see Elsie running toward him. He caught her in his arms.

"He's gone," he said. "I'm sorry."

Elsie said nothing, just cried. He held her tighter. What else was there to do, to say?

"I can't believe he hated me that much," she finally said and pulled back from him, searching his eyes.

"You weren't the problem. It was him. How anyone could care about their ambitions like that over other human beings…" Sure, people were selfish, but this was an extreme example. He had been a murderer, with seemingly no remorse. But now he was gone.

"He was my biological father," she said, still looking at him.

"I know."

"Does this change…? I mean, I know I messed up, Wyatt. I'm sorry about last night. If you ever forgive me for that, does it change how you feel, knowing…?" She trailed off and he put his hands on either side of her face, gently angled her to look at him.

"I love you, Elsie Montgomery. I know you. I know who you are, and *that* man does not define you."

"But knowing all of this…"

"It's only part of who you are in that it made you who you are. Let the past go, Elsie." He smiled a little. "Let's explore the future together."

"Are you going to propose again?" Her smile wavered a little.

"Only if you wouldn't turn me down this time," he teased back. "But you're right. I will wait. Let's get to know each other a little more."

"What if you change your mind and decide you don't love me as much as you thought when you get to know me?"

He pressed a kiss to her forehead and would have spoken, but a noise behind him caught their attention.

A helicopter was coming toward them, heading for the clearing in the woods. When it landed, troopers came out, guns at the ready.

Elsie and Wyatt put their hands up and Wyatt pointed at the unconscious man. "He's the only one left. Travis Cattleman threw himself off the cliff."

The next few minutes were spent sorting out taking the other man off to jail. He started to wake up as they loaded him in the helicopter and had to be restrained. He'd get plenty of years in prison for whatever role he had played in this, Wyatt was sure of it. Elsie would be really and truly free.

They could both face their future, together.

"You ready?" he asked Elsie before they stepped into the helicopter, Willow at their sides.

"If you're coming with me." She smiled at him, took his hand.

Wyatt knew he could promise that he would for the rest of his life. But that would wait. Today he would just keep getting to know her. Let her know him.

And they could keep falling a little more in love every day.

EPILOGUE

Six months later, Elsie was standing in the woods, Lindsay beside her.

"I can't believe you're marrying my brother," her friend teased. "And didn't tell me when it all happened."

Elsie laughed, reached down to pet Willow. "I didn't know how to tell you."

"Yeah, well, you're both fantastic people and it's about time you both found someone special enough to deserve you."

At her words, Elsie felt herself glow even more with love than she had a few minutes before. Lindsay's approval meant so much to her, not just because she was Elsie's best friend but because she was Wyatt's family. Reverend and Mrs. Chandler had made her feel the same way when they'd found out first about her relationship with Wyatt and then about their engagement. Elsie was part of their family, they'd said, and now it would be official.

She wasn't alone anymore. And better yet, she was with Wyatt, the only man who had ever made her feel like all her dreams were coming true. The man who knew the worst about her and loved her anyway.

The man who had led her to Jesus, who was changing her life a little more every day.

The man who'd stood by her through the scariest time in her life, when the man who had been her biological father fell off the cliff to his death. When she learned he'd killed her mother. When the troopers had told her they'd concluded their investigation and believed Travis had murdered Rebecca Reyes and indeed used the two women as bait to get Elsie somewhere where she was vulnerable, after his hired man failed to get her.

Music wafted through the spruce trees from the beach in front of her cabin, where she and Wyatt had chosen to get married. It was, after all, where everything had started between them, and it seemed fitting this should be where they made their vows to each other.

She could see them, Wyatt and Sven, both standing on the beach, waiting for her. Wyatt's dad was the pastor who would perform the ceremony. Willow would walk Elsie down the aisle.

As the music played, she walked toward the one she loved. They'd gone through some of the darkest times Elsie could imagine together. Now they were stepping into the future, as Wyatt liked to remind her, and as the sun shone on the rocky beach, dancing in glimmers of light off the waves, Elsie thought the future looked bright indeed.

"I love you," he whispered when she reached him and he took her hands in his.

"I love you, too." Elsie smiled back.

Elsie didn't register much of Wyatt's dad's words. She had eyes only for Wyatt, and it seemed he also had eyes only for her.

It was amazing to her that God had brought them to-gether, through all they'd both experienced.

And when Wyatt's dad finally told them to seal their love and vows with a kiss…

Elsie was only too happy to do so. Beside her, Willow barked. In the front row, Sven howled.

Wyatt and Elsie laughed. And then their lips met again as their happily-ever-after officially came true.

* * * * *

Dear Reader,

Thanks for reading Elsie and Wyatt's story! I had a fun time brainstorming and playing with ideas about Elsie's background. She fascinated me, this character who was so fiercely independent and yet vulnerable. She wants to know details about her own past, and to be understood by another person, even though it scares her. She wants to be known.

We all want to be known, don't we? I think God gave us this desire, every one of us. It's at the heart of the friendships we seek, the relationships we pursue. We want to be known fully and understood and still loved. I enjoyed exploring how this played out for Elsie, who didn't know who she was due to circumstances beyond her control. What I learned through writing this story is that maybe we won't ever truly understand ourselves. Maybe other people won't know and understand us as fully as we wish. But God does.

For Wyatt, being known meant letting his past go. Not being defined by it. I loved seeing how both characters' desires for connection drew them closer to God and to each other.

Thank you for reading this book and letting me share this story, and Alaska, with you! I love hearing from readers! You're welcome to find me on social media at Facebook. com/sarahvarlandauthor or on Instagram @sarahvarland, though I post entirely too many dog pictures. You can write me at sarahvarland@gmail.com.

Sarah Varland